Zombies,

Fireballs,

Snakes,

Death,

and Candy

by P.J. Stetson

Prologue

The plane exploded above the clouds. The flames were violent and the heat intense, but the debris was cowardly, fleeing the scene into the open sky below.

To the people of Coba, Indiana, the explosion was an odd piece of thunder, eluding its storm. Some of them stopped their activities, tilting their heads upward at the thick cloud canopy, darkening with the coming night, but others were too occupied to notice. They had good excuse.

Halloween.

Costumed children were too busy scurrying about with buckets in hand to stop and gawk for long. Some adults were handing out candy they had bought just hours ago at the Food O'Rama, while others were dressing for costume parties; all of them brushed off the sound as another oddity in the weirdest night of the year. The older children, free from adult-restraint, were having too much fun to notice, roaming the streets, arming themselves with eggs and toilet paper for mischief, or piloting the latest drones decorated as ghouls, witches, or UFOs.

On the outskirts of town, one of those older children, Quinn, was delicately piloting his UFO-shaped drone next to a squirrel skittering on an old oak tree. Blowing on the strand of white hair that fell from his George Washington wig, he worked the digital controls on his smart watch with expert finger movements. Trevor, Quinn's younger brother, who had definitely been adopted, was sneering in his villainous pirate costume, complete with fake parrot, black beard, and prosthetic hook.

"Yeth...yeth...," Trevor whispered with his teethy lisp, wringing his hand and hook together.

"Shh!" Quinn said for the third time.

Hovering as if on heavenly strings, the drone buzzed closer and closer to the curious squirrel; Quinn chewed on his lip, bringing the drone next to the squirrel's branch as stealthily as possible. Closer. Closer. Too close. The squirrel chittered and ran.

But just as Quinn was about to call it quits, the squirrel stopped and turned, its little paws drawn up and its nose twitching as it sniffed. Had it caught the acorn's scent?

"Come on, little guy," Quinn urged in a whisper.

The squirrel inched back toward the drone, pulled up cautiously, then jerked forward again, creeping closer to the drone and its bait. When it seemed to sense the drone was not an enemy, it leaped on top, snatching the acorn and triggering the trap. The cage slammed shut with a raging squirrel inside,

"YETH!" Trevor exclaimed.

But Quinn started to panic as the drone lurched uncontrollably with the additional weight. He fought with the controls, swiping his fingers back and forth, but the weight was too unbalanced for the drone. The squirrel was bouncing off the cage's walls like bursting popcorn, jerking the drone every which way. "I can't control it! It's…it's…"

The drone was drifting away, buzzing over the houses on the edge of town – but Quinn was no longer watching it. His fingers had frozen on the controls.

"Itth gettin' away!" Trevor shouted. "Itth ethcaping!"

Then Trevor caught sight of what Quinn was looking at. In the sky, beyond the drone. A shooting star. Or something like one. A streak of light and flame. A trail of smoke. Careening toward them.

2

"Oh no..."

And it struck the ground.

THHHHHHHH-UD!!

The object slammed into a barren cornfield beyond the oak tree. The boys shielded their eyes as dirt splashed their bodies. The sound – a simultaneous thud and crack – rang in their ears as little flecks of dirt rained on their costumes. Then there was nothing. No other sounds but their own hearts thumping up to their throats.

The boys exchanged looks, reluctant to turn their eyes toward the impact. Eventually their curiosity defeated their fear, and the cross-eyed pirate and white-haired revolutionary dashed toward the smoking earth, forgetting all about the floating squirrel prison.

The boys' hushed breaths quickened as they approached, padding through the dirt. "That was crazy," Quinn whispered to himself, as if whatever caused the impact could hear him. He shot glances at the town, but no one else was in sight. That could be a good thing – or, if the thing was dangerous – a really bad thing.

With each step, the crater before them seemed to grow deeper until finally, an object deep within the crater came into view. It appeared to be a broken crate, about the size of a coffin, made of some type of shiny material – crumpled, but not destroyed.

"Ith that what I think it ith?" Trevor asked.

"Probably not," Quinn muttered as he scooted closer to the hole's edge. "Probably not," he repeated, as if trying to give himself confidence to do what he was planning next. Once his confidence settled in, he took a deep breath and stepped over the edge.

He slid closer to the crumpled object as Trevor hollered at him from above. "It ith! Itth a treathure chetht!"

3

Quinn didn't reply this time. He was embarrassed that Trevor might be right for once. Anything with such a well-protected case *must* be of great value. Who knows what kind of treasure might be inside?

Leaning closer he saw some writing – a type of label, or a part of one that hadn't been burned to a flaky black coating of ash. "There's...there's some sort of label."

"Whath it thay?"

Quinn brushed away the ash and leaned in as close to the writing as he could, trying to piece the fragmented letters together. "Uh...Ant...Antiquity, I think...." He squinted. "And...Mayan. It says Mayan something."

Well, that rules out alien, he thought.

He lifted another ripped section, but it fell, disintegrating at his feet. Fortunately, he had read it just in time. His eyes darted along the object, at the broken lock, the crooked handle. The label had read: TOP SECRET. DO NOT OPEN.

But it was already open.

"What elth it thay?"

Quinn's mind buzzed with questions. Should he look inside? Should he report it to the authorities? Should he tell his parents? This was big. Bigger than some kids in Halloween costumes in fly-over country. This was national security. Huge. There would be people, powerful people, looking for this. And yet here he stood, the only one who knew where it was. It was as if this was his destiny – and not only his destiny – but the destiny of all kids who longed to have such opportunity. To be important. To know things.

He knew exactly what had to be done.

His hand reached out. His fingertips tested the handle's

temperature. Then he grasped it. He turned to Trevor. "You're not going to tell Mom, are you?"

Trevor smiled with his crooked teeth. "I get half."

Quinn smiled. "Deal."

He turned back to the case, took a deep breath, and opened it.

Chapter 1

One minute ago...

Declan spotted the monsters coming for the front door. They'd be there any moment now, expecting to eat. But they'd get more than what they came for.

He readied his gun.

DING-DONG!

Declan swung open the door and pointed the plastic gun at their chests.

"Trick-or-AAAGGHH!" the kids screamed.

Declan aimed at the monster to the left, a three-foot tall Star Wars creature. The one on the right was running away, but Declan could tell by the flailing tail that it had been a dinosaur of some sort. *Probably a Pansy-saurus. Or a Pterrified-dactyl.*

"Hand over the candy!" he commanded.

The kid-monster put its scaly arms on its green hips. "Who are you supposed to be?"

Declan smirked, straightened his clip-on tie, and pulled the gun back to his suited chest. "The name's Bond. Declan Bond," he said with a pump of his chin.

"Toy guns are s'posed to be off-limits this year."

Declan rolled his eyes. "Oh, yeah? You going to report me?"

The monster scoffed with an attitude, holding out its candy-collection bag. "Depends."

Declan couldn't help but laugh. This one had spunk. He turned and retrieved the candy he was supposed to be handing out and held it out with his gun hand, absent-mindedly pointing the gun at the monster.

BOOM!

The monster jerked with a yelp, dropping its candy. Declan looked at the gun in fright. So did the monster. Then he examined the monster's body. No holes. No blood. The sound hadn't come from the gun.

Other costumed children on the street were looking at the cloud-covered sky, as if the bang had come from above.

"What was that?" Declan asked, leaning out the doorway.

The monster didn't answer. In a flash, it had swiped its candy bag from the porch and waddled to the next yard.

After a long moment where the neighborhood seemed to have paused, everything began again, with parents escorting children on the sidewalks, cars inching along and kids excitedly sprinting from one house to the next. The thunderous sound was soon forgotten, even by Declan…after he checked down his gun barrel one last time.

"Declan!" his mother's voice beckoned from the upstairs.

"Wh-aaat?" he asked, annoyed even before she asked for something.

"Was that you banging around?"

"Just disposing of the bodies, Mother!"

"Okay. Well keep it down, will ya?"

Declan stomped toward the couch by the front window, kneeled on a cushion and peeked through the blinds, watching for his next victim. He waited impatiently, running his tongue along his large front teeth and wiping his silky bangs from his eyebrows. He tried not to think about his stupid twin brother going on some dumb mission with Trevor

– or about his friend, Carson, going trick or treating with his kinda-girlfriend, Kylie. He had better things to do anyway. This way he got all the candy he wanted, he told himself.

Then he saw her. She was floating down the sidewalk, graceful, light on her feet. Dressed in a powder-blue gown with lacy frills and a bonnet to match, it was easy to tell who she was supposed to be. The shepherd's hook in her hand made it even easier. And if there were still any question, she had brought a little lamb, a real live one, that waited patiently for her, tied to her pretty, white bicycle.

Little Bo Peep.

A really hot shepherdess.

Even though he knew who she was supposed to be, he had no idea who she really was. She was about Declan's age, so in a town this small, it was odd not to know who she was. Maybe she was new.

A new girl! If true, this would be their first interaction. And if he wanted there to be more than one interaction, his first one had to be spot on. First impressions were incredibly important for any future relationship. Most of the time girls didn't appreciate his first impressions, but someday he'd find a girl who was worthy of his efforts. And what better day than today – when he was wearing a suave suit and fancy tie?

As she approached the door, he knew he had the chance to woo her before she could be wooed by any other male in Coba, Indiana – including Carson, the accidental wooer of all females. There weren't many opportunities like this.

You can do it, Declan.

DING-DONG!

He whipped open the door with a smile that could melt the sun.

8

Then he pumped his chin and wiped his bangs away with a swipe of his gun. "The name's Bond..." he began.

"Bond! Can you please help me?" she pleaded with hands clasped in a begging motion. "I've lost my sheep and don't know where to find them."

Dang, she's beautiful. And quite the actress.

He choked on his words before regaining his silky composure. "Well, why don't you come in? Maybe we can find them at the bottom of a tall glass of Dr. Pepper."

A hint of a smile played on Bo Peep's gorgeous lips. And he couldn't help but notice her notice him. Unfortunately, she returned to character. "Sorry, Mr. Bond. I don't think they'd be inside a glass of Dr. Pepper. You sure you haven't seen them?"

Declan thought hard, then pointed his gun over her shoulder. "You know what? I think I see one. Fluffy white thing?"

Bo Peep followed his gaze to her sheep then jumped up and down in delight. "Thank you! Thank you! You found him!"

Declan laughed.

Then she hugged him.

Yep. She hugged him.

He didn't have time to open his arms. Instead, they were squished awkwardly in her embrace. Still, he didn't mind. She had hugged him.

Then she giggled, still in character, and pulled something out of a basket she'd left on the porch. It was a small paper plate with a slice of cake plastic-wrapped to it.

"As a token of my appreciation..."

Declan squinted. This was too good to be true. Was he dreaming? He reached out with his gun and poked the cake. It was squishy. "For real?"

She nodded, her bonnet bouncing. "It's angel-food cake."

Suddenly he was skeptical. Since when do beautiful girls show up on your doorstep, hug you, and give you cake? "Why you handing out cake? It's kind of donkey backward."

She shrugged and surrendered her character's bubbly smile. "Just to say thanks. I'm new here. Just moved in a few houses down. My dad's the new principal."

Declan cautiously took the cake from her. She was his neighbor? "Thanks," he said. "Want to…"

"You're welcome!" she replied. "Nice to meet you, Bond." Then before he could invite himself to go trick-or-treating with her, she turned on her heels and skipped away.

It only took a moment after the door closed for him to get his senses back. Of course, he watched her store the lamb in her bike's basket and ride off with her beautiful self, but then he flipped the porch light off to ward off any other intruders, ripped off the plastic wrap, threw his tie over his shoulder, and devoured the cake in the dark.

Ha! Who's the loser all alone on Halloween now? Not me. Hot-chick-hug and cake, baby!

He had just finished the cake and put his feet up when the door shot open and two shadowy figures darted inside.

Declan fumbled with his gun, but it flew uselessly into the air.

He rolled off the recliner, wielding the fork.

"Declan?" the shadowy figure whispered.

Declan recognized the boy's voice. His twin brother. "Quinn. What are you doing back?"

"THHHH!" Trevor whispered with serious spittle.

10

It was then that Declan saw Quinn more clearly. He was hunched over and dirty, holding onto some object like a running back with a golden football. His eyes were wide with fear; trails of sweat had formed little beads of mud below his white wig.

His twin brother used to look just like him, with matching long, blonde haircut and chubby cheeks. The major difference between them had been his bigger front teeth. But then, something had happened in sixth grade. Quinn had cut his hair, lost weight, and lost interest in being like Declan. Declan had acted like he didn't care, but there had been something more than similar looks that had been lost.

Pirate Trevor, their adopted brother, was right behind Quinn, checking their backs as he clicked the front door locked with his hook. Trevor didn't look anything like the twins. He was shorter, stouter, and had a crazy mess of permanent bedhead. And he had a lazy eye with a mind of its own. Declan felt bad for the kid sometimes, when he wasn't annoying the heck out of him.

"What is it?" Declan asked, squinting at the muddy, disc-shaped object in Quinn's arms. It was possibly made of stone – like the top section of a bird bath or a pizza statue. But who had bird baths anymore?

"I don't know," Quinn said, panting and peeking out the blinds. Then he darted toward the basement door. "But it's Mayan."

Declan scoffed. "Well, geez, you could *share*."

Quinn made a face as he swung open the basement door. For a moment it looked like he wanted to say something – some sort of witty put-down – but he just shook his head and set off. Trevor followed close at Quinn's heels as the door clicked closed behind them.

Declan furrowed his brow, alone again. "O-kaaay."

11

What were his weirdo brothers up to? Sure, Quinn often did weird-nerd things like geo-caching and Trevor did weird-*stupid* things like making a helmet out of banana peels.

But this…*this* was different. They were doing something together. Something serious. And they had looked scared.

Declan, on the other hand, didn't scare easily. He'd seen enough science fiction movies, horror movies, and teachers' lounges that nothing could shake him anymore. His school counselor labeled him 'desensitized.' His mom called him calloused. But whatever it was, he was ready for whatever the world threw at him.

In fact, he felt that if something really deserving of his fright would actually happen to him – in Coba, Indiana – that he would just point and laugh. A spaceship landing. *Ha – nice special effects!* A werewolf under his bed – *good doggy*! Or a zombie apocalypse – *where's my chainsaw?*

So, seeing Quinn and Trevor all flustered may have intrigued him, but it didn't scare him. Rather, it just pestered him enough to prompt fleeting glances to the basement door every now and then – between scaring trick-or-treaters.

He had almost forgotten them when it happened.

A bang, flashing lights, and a sharp, eerie whistle broke the silence. Declan leapt from the couch in a panic. The plastic gun clattered to the floor, and Declan landed next to it as he slid down, hiding from whatever had made the noise. Huddling close to the couch's bottom, he crawled to a gap between it and a recliner, not even noticing that their cat, Pawl, was hiding along with him. Their two bodies barely fit, but neither thought to escape as the lights and whistles continued assaulting the room.

When he peeked out, he saw the source of the commotion.

The basement door was vibrating, pulsing with a green energy that outlined its frame. There were other noises. Voices, maybe – coming from the basement. But those were muffled by the throbbing whistle that stung his eardrums.

And then it was gone. The green light, the whistle, the voices – all of it was gone, leaving only a ringing in Declan's ears as a trace of its existence.

"Declan! Turn down that TV!" came his mother's bellow from upstairs.

Even *her* voice was muffled by the intense ringing in his ears.

He rubbed them, grimacing as he replied. "It was *QUINN!*"

"Just keep it down!"

Declan rolled his eyes at Pawl as he shooed him away before emerging from their hiding place. Poking fingers in his ears and working his jaw, he took a moment to collect his thoughts. He peeked outside, only seeing a few curious eyes looking toward his house. But if there were any day where strange noises coming from houses didn't raise red flags, Halloween was it. There were weirder houses on the same block – with ghosts in the trees, haunting shrieks from sound machines, and witches in rocking chairs.

Maybe that was it. Maybe Quinn and Trevor had stolen some Halloween effects machine. That would explain the sounds *and* their secrecy.

And…if it were true…Quinn should be busted. He never got caught doing anything wrong! It wasn't fair! Sure, he never *did* anything wrong, but still…

A mischievous smile played on Declan's face as he marched to the basement door. But before he opened it, he took out his phone and started recording video. If Quinn was doing something wrong, he would need hard-core evidence to convict him in his mother's eyes.

Pumping his eyebrows at the camera, he grasped the doorknob.

It was time to bring Quinn down a few notches – closer to where Declan was permanently notched below all other notches.

He swung open the door and barreled down the stairs.

Chapter 2

Declan clamored down the wooden stairs, squinting as his eyes adjusted to the dark, and swung his camera toward the cluttered room. He caught them red-handed. Or green-handed, really. Quinn and Trevor both tugged on a muddy disc that glowed with green jewels around its perimeter. The light shone on their pale skin, mixing with the light from a dim bulb hanging above the card table. The table sat in the middle of the concrete floor – an island surrounded by boxes, chests, Christmas decorations, mannequins, and other weird things the boys had collected and neglected over the years.

Quinn and Trevor stopped jostling when they saw Declan, but neither relented their grip on the disc. "Declan, turn that off," Quinn muttered in a hushed whisper.

Declan watched him on his phone-camera's screen. "No. The cops will want to see this."

"The cops?"

"Yeah. You know. The ones you usually call on me?"

Quinn suddenly let go of the disc, and Trevor yelped as it ricocheted against his nose.

"OW! My nothe!"

The twins ignored Trevor's pain.

"I'm serious, Declan. *THIS* is serious," Quinn urged, pointing at the glowing disc in Trevor's hands.

Declan rolled his eyes. "I know. Like a serious *misdemeanor.* Stealing lawn decorations isn't the coolest crime out there; but you're not the coolest *anything*, so I guess it makes…"

Quinn pushed out of his chair and took a big step toward Declan. Declan retreated a step, taken aback by his brother's intensity.

"This isn't a lawn decoration. It's…it's…something…"

"Ah…"

"…something powerful. When Trevor licked it, it lit up and…"

"Licked it?" Declan asked, grimacing at Trevor.

Trevor shrugged, still holding the disc that had just struck his nose. "I wath claiming it." Then he sniffed, wiping at his nose with his hooked hand; his hook came up bloody.

Declan was about to say something witty, but he stopped mid-breath, watching with disgust as Trevor tried to wipe the blood from his nose with every spare piece of clean cloth and skin he had on him.

Still ignoring Trevor, Quinn took a final step and pressed Declan's phone camera down. His voice was quiet but weighty – in a serious tone that Declan could never manage. "Listen. It was in a chest that fell from the sky. It was labeled *Top Secret* and said something about being Mayan. The chest was the size of a coffin, but only had this in it. *Only* this." His bespectacled eyes were large with passion. "*Think* about it. This is big – important! And it just fell from the sky right next to me. Like *destiny*. Like it *wanted* to come to me. So we have to keep it hidden. From the government. Mom."

Declan had fallen into a mesmerized stupor, trying to wrap his fragile mind around the situation. But he couldn't hold his concentration. Not when Trevor was blowing his nose on the top-secret powerful disc.

"Sick!" he exclaimed as Trevor let out another farmer-blow, releasing a globule of blood and snot onto the disc.

Declan's eyes fell on the disk where, almost imperceptibly, a tiny

16

drop of blood pooled in a smooth channel, wound toward the center, and was sucked inside.

The green jewels suddenly went dark. The green light was gone. The disc was dead.

Only the dim, yellowing light bulb lit their startled faces.

A deep silence settled into the room. There were usually creaks and groans from the furnace, the water heater, or whatever, but now there was nothing but the pressure in Declan's ears. It was almost as if he were underwater.

And then his hand started on fire.

"Yow!" he yelped as he dropped the flaming phone to the ground and swiped his hot hand across his suit.

At the same time, the light bulb above the table burst into glass shards that glimmered in the lingering firelight coming from the burning phone. The fragments tinkled in all directions, spattering Declan's face and hair. Finally, there was a muffled thrum, thrum, thrum and a crackle of sparks coming from outside.

It had all happened in a short few seconds, but the shock lasted much longer. The boys were frozen in their places. Only Declan moved at all, massaging his hand as the heat dissipated.

Quinn was the first to move, rushing toward the basement's only window and pulling back the black curtain. As Declan and Trevor both rushed to join him, they saw the last few lights down the street blink out in a show of sparks. Darkness. Only shadows in moonlight.

"Whoa," Trevor exclaimed as the darkness that had started inside their little basement bunker descended on the entire town.

The twins eyed each other, their widened eyes glowing with the moon's light. Their eyes also held a sense of wonderment and realization behind them. They knew what had caused the disruption. But they couldn't believe it – even with the understanding that it had to be true.

And then their eyes began to take on another glow. A green glow. Faint at first, but feathering into brighter hues, as if a green pool were bubbling and sparkling from within the basement walls, reflecting in their pupils.

They turned at the same time, their mouths agape.

Chapter 3

The disc was hovering in the air, its green jewels ebbing in and out as if the disc had a pulse. The low thrumming sound was its heartbeat, giving it life – a frightening, powerful life with a single dominating eye staring the boys down without a blink.

Declan gaped at Quinn and then back at the thing, hovering in place. Was it Sauron from Lord of the Rings? If so, it was the single coolest Halloween prop ever made. Maybe Declan wouldn't turn Quinn in to the cops after all. Well, at least until they got good use out of it...

And then it spoke. "I AM DOOM!"

The male voice thumped in their chests, rattled the glass fragments on the floor, and blew their eyelids back into their skulls. They scooted their backs against the wall, and Trevor snuck behind them, cowering. The thing could talk! It could blow up light bulbs, light phones on fire, and *talk*. For a moment, Declan finally felt a twinge of fright.

"I AM THE ENDER OF WORLDS!"

The fright left Declan as quickly as it had come. It was all too much. Too extravagant to be real. But it was pretty amazing. "Really? The ender of worlds, huh?"

The disc's lights twinkled as if the thing was thinking.

"Yes. I am the ender of them," it explained without yelling.

Declan snorted. "No, really. Who is this? A drone with a speaker? And an EMP? This is like legit technology!"

The disc's jewels blinked rapidly. "You dare doubt me, human? Were you not impressed with my impairment of your pathetic city's power grid?"

"City? Coba isn't a city. It has like two stoplights," Declan stated. Of course, he had been impressed by the display. But if the disc-thing wanted to convince him that it had the power to end worlds, it had a lot of work to do.

"Do you need a greater display? How about your state's power grid? Done. Congratulations! You just turned a million televisions off in the middle of the *Simpsons Halloween Special*. Oh, and I can see the panic in the eyes of hundreds of dying hospital patients. Good thing they have back up generators or you would be responsible for the deaths of thousands of your fellow humans. But…I guess there is still time. One hour to be exact."

Declan shook his head in disbelief – and annoyance. "How do you get your voice to sound so real? I don't even see speakers. Who is this for real?"

"I AM DOOM! THE ENDER OF WORLDS! Geez! You would think thousands of years of evolution would have achieved a minor bump in your species' intelligence…but no. The humans who finally figure out how to wake me from my slumber – the ones who I would think are the cream of the crop – are nothing but the cream of the *slop*. Imbeciles. Especially you, Declan."

The boys were dumbstruck as the disc continued its rant.

"And yes, I know your name. Declan Michael Finneman. Twin brother of Quinnton Thomas Finneman. You were born first – a full three minutes before Quinn, and with a full twenty points lower IQ – which isn't saying much – because all humans are dumber than my left pinky's fingernail – if I had one. Do you still doubt me, Declan? Do you want to hear more?"

Trevor jumped in. "Yeth!"

"Declan, you wipe with your left hand, your phone's password is one two three four, and you spend roughly 21.32349 minutes on your hair each morning...and 5.16784 at night."

Declan shrugged, trying to hide his amazement. "Everyone knows that..."

Quinn whispered. "But you should really shut the door when you poop."

"And be stuck in my own stink?"

The disc thrummed louder. "Well, Declan, does everyone know whose picture you hide under your bed?"

Declan drew back. "How do you know...?"

"Do you still doubt my powers? Or should I say more?"

After a long pause, Declan sighed. It was clear: the disc, or whoever was controlling it, was beyond powerful. It was like a know-it-all in a snarky, yet true kind of way. And that was scary. "I don't doubt you, Almighty Frisbee," he finally blurted. "Do you, Quinn? Trevor?"

They both shook their heads, gulping their fear.

"Good," said the Frisbee.

"But," Declan interjected despite an elbow-poke from Quinn. "Besides being a super-powerful Frisbee – who are you? Are you like an A.I., or an alien...or an alien god?"

"It would take too long to explain it to you dimwitted morons. All that you need to know is that I have unimaginable power. And don't call me Frisbee."

"Alright, Discus. Then why are you here?"

"Do you not listen? Ugh...!" Discus turned in mid-air, as if it couldn't bear to look at him any longer. "Why teenagers? Of all the despicable creatures to deal with...I am Doom – the Ender..."

"…of Worlds!" Declan butted in. "I know…but…." It finally dawned on him. The meaning of his name. "OH! You're here to end the world?"

The disc swiveled back, slowly. "Yes…*you idiot.*"

Declan acted offended. "You call me Idiot, I'll call you Frisbee."

"Did you miss the part about me being unimaginably powerful? I will call you Idiot – because that is what you are. And you will call me by my name, because that…"

Declan sighed. "Fine. How about Ender? The other stuff is just too long."

"Yes, too many syllables and Declan's mind starts drifting off to dinosaurs and legos…"

"Why?" Quinn chimed impatiently.

There was a long pause. Declan had thought Quinn too frightened to speak, but his voice said otherwise.

"Well, because Declan's brain has the capacity of a five-year-old."

"No," said Quinn. "Well…maybe…but I want to know why – why you want to end the world."

"Because," said the Frisbee, "it's what I was created to do - my purpose. When I am wakened by blood, I give the world one hour to save itself from complete destruction."

The boys shared a desperate look. Declan lost all desire to be witty. For the first time, he thought maybe the disc could be telling the truth. How else would it know all about him? How else would it control electricity? Who knows what it was or who had created it? Did it matter?

What *did* matter was stopping it.

But he wasn't the one to do it. Where was Carson when he needed him? Carson was the brave one. Or for that matter – the cops, the

22

military, the adults in general! They all needed to know that this thing intended on ending the world.

Quinn was one step ahead of him – as always. "You said we can save ourselves?" Quinn asked. "How?"

"I'm glad you asked. Now I can get to the point, eliminate your world, and go back to sleep without you annoying dimwits bugging me. So listen close, because I will only say this once. I will not explain myself or answer any stupid questions after. If you fail to follow these instructions, humanity is doomed."

"You sound like my teacher," Declan piped.

Ender sighed in annoyance. "I should have lit your phone on fire when it was *in* your pocket. Now shut up and listen. Ready?" Ender made the sound of clearing his throat.

Quinn held a finger to his lips with one hand and held Trevor back with the other – keeping him from doing anything stupid. "Don't…make…a noise," he muttered just before Ender's jewels went dark. Then, as if signaling the start of the clock, the disc's top-most light lit up.

The boys held their collective breath as his all-important message began.

"All civilization must face a test. Only the worthy survive. Those who hear this message are the Chosen Few. It was you who woke Doom – the Ender of Worlds. Now only you can save your world. From this very second, you have one hour to deliver a pure, white sac – "

"DECLAN! ARE YOU DOWN THERE?"

His mom's voice echoed from the stairway above, sending the boys into barely constrained panic. Their eyes were wide with intense focus, as if staring at the disc would help them hear its words.

"...delivering it to me without blemish within the hour. With every passing ten minutes, a new catastrophe will befall humanity. The first will..."

"THERE ARE TRICK-OR-TREATERS AT THE DOOR!"

"...the second will come from the sky, the third from the sea, the fourth from the earth, and the fifth from the..."

"GET UP HERE NOW!"

"Pipe down, Mom!" Declan bellowed back.

"...sixth will be the end of all things. And only you will be to blame. You have fifty-nine minutes remaining."

Chapter 4

The disc fell to the card table with a deep thud, all but one of its lights completely out.

As the disc wobbled on the table like a giant quarter, the boys were still in shock, struck immobile by thoughts both of impending doom and desperate confusion. *What now?* seemed to be the silent refrain.

"So…," Declan began, "Did you guys get that?"

"No!" Quinn burst out in frustration. "I didn't. Trevor?"

Trevor shook his head no, still peeking timidly at the disc.

"Great," Declan sighed. "We're dead. Dead! All of us. Humanity. Dead because of a nagging mother."

Quinn took in a deep breath and sat on one of the chairs, eyeing the disc. "We're not dead. Not yet anyway." He glanced at his smart watch, which still shone with the time. "We have an hour."

Declan nodded into a reverie, whispering to himself. "An hour to live. One hour…"

He began to take off his suit coat.

Quinn had been studying the disc for thirty seconds before he turned to see Declan rustling through an old dusty box labeled 'Video Games.' "Wh..wh…what are you doing?"

"What? An hour to live – and I'm a boy of my word."

Quinn was speechless.

"What?" Declan asked. "I said I would beat Halo 5 on legendary if it was the last thing I'd do. Now it's the last thing I'll do so…"

Trevor spoke for Quinn. "This is therieuth."

"Yeah," Quinn agreed. "You heard Ender. We only have ten minutes before some sort of catastrophe. We might be able to stop it if – maybe all of us together can remember what he said, okay? We have to try!"

Trevor took a seat next to Quinn, a determined look in his roving eye. "We are the Chothen Few."

Declan rolled his eyes. "Fine. But we have no idea what he said. 'We need to bring him something?' Great. That narrows it down."

"He said something pure and white…and without blemish," Quinn recalled out loud.

Declan closed the video game box with a cloud of dust, letting Quinn do the thinking.

"It was something that began with 'sa.' Did anyone hear the rest? Sa…sa…"

Trevor jolted up from his seat. "Thacofrithe!"

Declan leaned against the box, stunned. Trevor wiped his nose with his hook. And Quinn pushed his spectacles further up his nose in a self-satisfied revelation. "Are you sure, Trevor?"

Trevor gave a sturdy nod.

Quinn nodded back, resolute. "Makes sense. He needs a pure, white, unblemished…*sacrifice*."

The uttered word sank heavy in the musty basement air. In some boys' minds it would bring images of sacrificial pop flies in baseball stadiums. But in most minds, including Declan's, it brought to mind pictures of knives and altars and blood. Sacrifice was a heavy word with frightening implications.

"So…we need to kill somebody? Or one of us?" Declan asked.

"You can relacth," Trevor said. "He wanth thumbody pure and unblemithed."

Declan sneered as hard as he could and held up a fist.

26

"Guys, think," Quinn redirected. "Ender said we need to deliver it within an hour. Deliver *it*. So not a person, right? Ender would have said 'he' or 'she'."

"Or maybe he meant a body..." Declan replied with a shrug.

Quinn's brow creased. "True. I hope it...it couldn't expect us to...?" he asked no one in particular, clenching his teeth in frustration. "Never mind that for now. What is pure and white? Name things. Anything or anyone."

"Coconut," Trevor blurted. "Vanilla yogurt. Ithe cream. Mayonnaithe. Thwith cheethe...," he said with a crooked-teethed smile.

As Trevor went on, Declan dusted off his shirt and noticed a stain on it. It looked like a cake-stain. And then it struck him.

His eyes darted back and forth in memory as his heart raced to catch up. Something had just happened to him. It was wonderful. A warm, satisfying feeling in his chest, inflating it with hope and confidence. He had had...*an idea*.

"A lamb," he said, as if the word itself was spirit.

"Huh..." Quinn thought out loud. "A lamb...of course! They used to sacrifice lambs in biblical times. The blood was supposed to cover their sins...to save them from God's wrath!"

"I know," Declan huffed, even though it was obvious he didn't. "That's why I said it. And I happen to know where one is. Or was..."

Quinn waited with an extended shrug. "And where...?"

"It's Little Bo Peep's. She's the new girl. Totally hot, by the way! Like smoking, okay? She came to the door and was all over me. Hugged me like three-and-a-half seconds. Then she told me where she lived and gave me cake."

Trevor slurped excess saliva. "Ith there any left?"

"No. Duh."

Quinn was biting his lip, contemplating the thought.

"Doth the girl have any more cake?" Trevor asked.

"Not for you."

Trevor snorted. "Do you even know her name?"

Declan balked, searching his memory. "Our connection is deeper than names."

"You're making thith up."

"Am not!"

"Are to!"

"Am not!"

"Then let me thmell your breath."

"My breath? Why?"

"It'll thmell like cake. If you're telling the truth…"

"Fine!" Declan opened his mouth and breathed hard on Trevor's face.

Quinn rested his head against the disc with a frustrated sigh and a loud bump. The other two boys turned to him as he took off his glasses and rubbed his eyes. The poor kid was overwhelmed.

As much as Quinn frustrated Declan, Declan also cared for him in a kind of way where it sucked to see him get hurt or cry. It had been that way as long as he could remember. He would hit Quinn, being angry as ever at him, then Quinn would cry and everything would change. Suddenly he wanted to hug him and make it up to him. Maybe it was a twin thing…or just a brother thing.

"What's wrong, bro?" Declan asked, pushing Trevor away from his mouth.

"What's wrong? What's *wrong*?" Quinn asked, looking around the room in a wild-eyed manner. "The world is going to end and we're talking about cake. That's what's wrong!"

Declan wiped glass fragments from the chair next to his brother's and sat. Putting his hand on Quinn's back, Declan took a moment to let out a long, drawn-out sigh. "It's okay, dude. We'll be fine." He patted his back. "You'll get us out of this."

Quinn blinked and blinked again, staring at the wall in disbelief.

Trevor sat down, too, adding his own encouragement. "Yeah. What he thaid."

With a grieving moan, Quinn dropped his shaking head toward the table again. Then his eyes went wide and his hand snapped his glasses back to his eyes. He was squinting at the disc near its only glowing light, his finger pointing at something etched in the stone exterior.

"Look at this!" he exclaimed.

The other two boys rushed to look over his shoulder. Declan saw the etchings clearly. A circle connected to a vertical line below, with two lines branching to the right and two more branching below. In the middle of the circle were two small 'X'es.

"Is that a…?" Quinn asked.

Declan's lips curled into a smile as he recognized the human stick figure with its arms outstretched in front of it and its eyes as dead as its body.

"A zombie," Declan whispered in reverence.

And just as he said it, a second light lit up, a deep THRUM echoed in the room, shaking the glass on the floor, and the zombie etching took on a red hue. Quinn pushed his chair away from the disc and the others gaped in fear. The resounding THRUM was gone as fast as it

29

had come, but it still played in their ears, like a gong had been struck under their feet.

They braced themselves for more. For the catastrophe that had been promised. They waited with bated breaths.

But nothing else happened.

Declan gulped loud enough for the others to hear. "See? It's all some sort of prank. I mean, I can draw a better zombie than that."

Quinn finally breathed again in deep heaves. A new resolve seemed to come over him as he peered again at the disc. "But a second light lit up. That must mean it's been ten minutes…so that must have been the first catastrophe. Whatever it was."

"A giant prank – that's what it is. And a good one! Where are the hidden cameras? Seriously!" He started rummaging around the boxes in the dark, checking the wooden beams above and every crevice he could see.

"Declan. I'm as skeptical as anyone, but this…this is real. And we have to do something. We have ten minutes before the next…" he drew away as he spoke, looking again at the disc, "…it looks like a rock that's on fire. Like a meteor," he added, running his finger on the second etching.

Declan ignored him, stepping up on a pile of boxes, crunching in their tops to reach the ceiling – where he'd found a knot in the floorboards above. Searching for a hidden camera, he stuck a finger in the dark hole.

CREAK…

He drew back his hand as the sound sucked the air from the room. Quinn and Trevor turned their gazes toward the ceiling.

There were more creaks and distant thuds, like footsteps.

Lumbering footsteps.

Creak...creak...cre-eeeeeak.

Declan held his breath, his rapt attention on the noise upstairs. His eyes darted, lost in his own imagination. An imagination that drew frightening pictures.

Then came the screams.

The boys gasped and shot looks toward the source – the dark window to the street.

Declan's heart thudded against his ribs as the screams continued.

Then there was scratching on the floor above, a hissing, animal-like yelp that sped above them toward the basement door.

Had he left the door open? He searched his memory as he clambered down from the boxes.

In the chaos, he caught a glimpse of Trevor peering through the window, his face locked in bewilderment and then horror. No words came from his open mouth. But Declan didn't have time to ask what he was seeing. He had to close the door to keep whatever was upstairs from coming down.

He raced to the bottom of the steps as the thing raced down.

Meee-RAWR!

Pawl scrambled to find footing on the basement's concrete, his claws scratching at the smooth surface as he slid against the wall in absolute fright. Finally gathering his footing, he zipped through Declan's legs and slammed into a hole in the boxes, scrummaging as deep as he could get.

Even before Declan could swallow the apple-sized lump in his throat, the lumbering footsteps creaked in the floor above. Louder, heavier.

And the screams intensified outside. It was children screaming bloody murder.

It was all too much to take in. The boys were frozen in fear, their minds battling to find something, anything that they could do. Part of Declan wanted to crawl in the hole with Pawl the cat, but another part was slapping that idea down.

Instead, his eyes trailed up the stairs to the door above. It was cracked open, light coming in from the kitchen. The footfalls were closer now.

He didn't know if he could beat it there. He was afraid. Too scared to confront what he knew to be up there.

So he turned around, looking over Trevor and now Quinn's shoulders as they gaped out the window. Kids were running past. A car crashed into a light pole, shattering its glass on the street. And the screams continued. One scream stopped suddenly, leaving the reason why to his imagination.

CREAK!

He turned back to see the light eclipsed by a dark shadow. It was a human figure. Slouched. Limbs flopped at its sides, and its head lolled to one side. Its raspy moans grew louder and louder until it finally came into view.

"M...Mom?"

His mom pressed herself through the door with her shoulder.

Declan couldn't find enough breath in his deflated lungs. He wanted to warn the others but was stuck. Maybe he wasn't as de-sensitized as he had thought. This was too much for even him. His own mom, with lifeless eyes, drooling, moaning. Her gray flesh was rotting, nearly falling off her face. Though she drove him crazy, obviously played favorites, and had given up on his biological dad, he still loved her. He loved her more than anyone, though he'd never admit it – even to himself.

And now here she was. Undead. Hungry.

But then he sensed Quinn at his side. And it only took a moment for him to react.

"Declan! Run!" Quinn pulled on his arm just as their undead mother toppled down the stairs.

Chapter 5

The tumbling zombie mother crashed toward them like a lopsided wrecking ball, her flailing limbs doing nothing to slow her fall. Her moaning ragdoll body was almost upon Declan when he finally darted away, dragged by Quinn to the basement's interior.

"Quick! Make a barricade!" Quinn yelled.

And like that, Declan was primed for action. The three boys turned over the table and chairs, throwing them at the collapsed body at the foot of the stairs. They ransacked the boxes and storage containers – an old crib, a broken ironing board, a tricycle – anything they could find was sent toward the pile.

"Block her in!"

Their zombie mother let out a loud groan as she managed to stand. One of her arms was broken, twisted in a way it shouldn't go, and her teeth were nearly gone. Her eyes, deep and sunken into pits now, locked onto Declan's. She let out a raspy growl.

And then a paint can pummeled her nose, sending her stumbling backward.

Declan saw that it was Trevor chucking the cans. Sure, the impact had given them another precious second... but it was their *mom*.

Declan knocked the next can out of Trevor's hands, splattering the wall with blood-red paint. All it took was a glare. The next thing Trevor grabbed was softer.

Despite the growing pile, Mom pressed forward, pushing at the pile, making a path. It was then Declan realized they were trapped. Their only routes out – the window or the stairs – were behind the flesh-eating zombie. And they were trapping her there.

Or at least they were trying.

Suddenly the zombie was crawling over the first heap and rolling down.

Declan made a glance at the staircase. Could they get past her? Or would they have to fight? Would they have to…attack her? *Kill* her?

He'd seen enough zombie movies to know that he would have to puncture her brain to kill her. But how could he do that to his mother?

The short answer was that he couldn't. And he knew it. They would have to find another way. Restrain her? Distract her?

This time he went rummaging in the pile looking for something specific. Something that would occupy her just long enough for them to escape. Something she would want more than their flesh.

He threw Pawl at her despite his rabid shrieks. The cat's claws raked the air and then the zombie's face as the two creatures latched onto each other.

As soon as Declan saw the successful throw, he knew this was their only chance. "Go! Now!"

Quinn was a step ahead, leaping to the disc and snatching it up before stomping around the feasting zombie, clambering over the pile, and jumping down to the foot of the stairs. As the other two raced up the stairs, Declan looked back to see his mother begin to eat all of Pawl's nine-lives.

He gagged, imagining the hairball that his zombie mother would have to cough up. Then, before he sprinted after Quinn and Trevor, he gave a quick salute, thanking Pawl for finally doing something useful.

Ten seconds later he arrived at the front door, panting heavy, grasping at the back of Quinn's shirt to keep from falling over. "Slow

35

down, nerd. We'll need to save our energy."

Quinn's voice was unfazed by Declan's insult. "This is insane."

Declan immediately saw what he meant. Chaos in the streets. There were zombies everywhere. One zombie, still in its head-to-toe wizard costume had pinned a boy on the front lawn across the street. The boy's superman outfit didn't give him enough strength to pry himself free. Another zombie chased a few kids until they managed to get inside the car that had plowed into a light pole. They closed the door just in time, but they hadn't noticed the driver had turned to zombie. The kids had nowhere to run.

It didn't take long for Declan to realize that it had been the adults to turn. And as far as he could tell, it had been all of them – all at once.

"We have to do something," Quinn muttered, still helpless in the doorway. He turned, staring accusingly at Declan. "Believe it's real yet?"

Declan's heart broke even as his brain spun. This was real. And it was a full-blown zombie apocalypse. Guiltily, he realized he had been waiting for this day ever since binge-watching *The Walking Dead*. Why had he longed for it? Maybe there was something about seeing the world in a mess that made him almost giddy. Maybe it was the collapse of all the structure, all the rules and authority that stifled him. Or maybe it was the license to kill that seemed to quench his thirst for power.

But now, seeing firsthand the real pain and suffering zombies caused, and knowing that somewhere out there was a hot sheep-herder in a frilly blue dress who was probably in trouble, he was motivated as ever to kill as many zombies as he could. And with his knowledge, he was uniquely prepared to lead the charge. Years of zombie movie binge-watching would finally pay off. For once, he was smarter about something than Quinn was. This was his chance to step up, to be the older brother, and lead.

"Ok, guys. Listen. We have to figure out if they're all the type of zombie Mom is. If they're Walking Dead, like her, they're slow and we can deal. If there are some like World War Z or 28 Days Later, we...well, we gotta run for it. Mom was definitely a slow one, but can't say they'll all be that way. And we need to figure out if they're drawn by sound, by smell of our blood, or both. But first, we need weapons..."

"We have to help them..." Quinn muttered to himself, cutting Declan off. He turned back just before running out. "We have to help them!"

Before Declan could stop him, Quinn was sprinting toward the smoking car, Trevor close at his heels.

Surprise choked the word "WAIT!" from Declan's throat as he stood in the doorway, both wisdom and cowardice weakening his legs. He had serious arguments, good reasons not to rush head long into the zombie apocalypse without any weapons or strategy, but he knew why Quinn had made his decision.

Looking to Quinn's destination, Declan caught sight of the kids in the car, pressed against the window, sheer terror on their faces. The zombie in the driver's seat was lunging, snapping at them, but its seat belt kept it at bay. Its hands were free to grab at the kids, though, and it was only a matter of time before it grabbed a loose layer of clothing and pulled one of their little bodies close enough for rabid, salivating teeth to find flesh.

And then there was the zombie pounding the window, just inches from the children's screaming faces on the other side. Would it be strong enough to break through?

Finally, there was the smoke pluming from the car's hood. Its engine

37

was on fire. How long until the fire spread to the gas tank?

No wonder Quinn was in such a hurry.

But Declan wasn't in a hurry to die.

He turned to the living room, eyes searching for a weapon. Anything could be a weapon if used correctly. Well, maybe not a couch cushion. A coat hanger? A piece of broken glass?

He heard Quinn's shouting voice and turned to see him wrangling with the zombie outside the car. Trevor knelt on all fours behind the zombie, and Quinn pushed hard. The zombie toppled over the table-top maneuver just as their spontaneous plan must have called for. Except Quinn toppled with it, falling just feet from the angry creature. It grabbed at Quinn's leg and Quinn kicked back, but the zombie was unaffected, unfeeling, unrelenting. And worse, the commotion was bringing more their way. The wizard zombie had finished with Superman; now he lumbered toward the flaming car.

Declan had no time. He had to get something – anything!

And then he saw it.

In just a few seconds, he was sprinting outside holding his weapon above his head – a staff made of a curtain rod, with a flowing cape made of curtains waving behind. He first planned to whack the zombie's head with it, but once he'd seen how Quinn's kicks had failed to stop it, a new idea struck him.

Just as the zombie pulled Quinn's calf toward its jaws, its rotten teeth found curtain rod instead. Its teeth broke, rattling on the street as it continued biting the rod, all while Declan jumped on its back, looping the curtains and tying the zombie's arms behind its back. Quinn whimpered, kicking free as the muzzled zombie slobbered and growled, chomping at its bit with Declan's mass holding it down.

In another moment, Declan had finished the knot with a mighty pull. "It's curtains for you!"

Still crab-walking away, Quinn first looked at Declan in astonishment and then down to the zombie who was writhing on the asphalt, disabled by the curtain rod in his mouth and the attached curtains tied around its arms and neck. It was nothing but a helpless, very-angry worm now.

"Really?" came Ender's voice from the street where he had been dropped. "*Curtains for you?*"

Declan heaved in exertion, swallowing large gulps of adrenaline and fear. But then he smiled smugly. He had saved them. He had been the hero. Nothing could take that away now.

"RAHHH!" a costumed zombie rasped as he rounded the car's hood and zeroed-in on Quinn's back.

Quinn's face turned to horror as he swiveled to face the noise of the wizard zombie. It was almost upon him. Somehow its thick, broken glasses had managed to stay on its rotting nose, and its blood-red scarf matched the color of its lips and teeth. It had just fed on something. And now it was looking to feed again.

Declan would be too late this time.

Chapter 6

Suddenly, the wizard-zombie's head jerked back as if a lightning bolt had struck its forehead. The zombie's magic wand flapped uselessly in the air as it sputtered and moaned. It lingered on its feet for a moment, wavering as if magic kept it levitating for one last moment.

Declan gulped in air, still too frightened to move.

Finally, the wizard twisted and fell to the street where deep, black goo dripped from a circular hole in its forehead.

"Get up!" rang a familiar voice.

Declan turned to see a boy his age wearing a tan fedora and a weathered satchel running toward them. His green eyes were fierce and determined.

Carson. He held a slingshot in one hand while the other yanked Declan to his feet. Behind him was a girl dressed as some sort of jockey in high black boots, a frame-hugging equestrian jacket, and a trim black helmet. *Kylie.* She passed Carson, speeding to the car door instead.

The kids.

Kylie whipped the door open and accepted the boy and girl in a giant hug as the zombie driver's throaty gasps grew louder and more desperate. In a few harried moments, they had snatched up Ender and ushered the kids to the safety of the twins' doorway, looking through curtainless windows as the car burst into flames.

The zombie inside roasted, still reaching toward them with flames wrapping around it, its melting flesh dripping in thick chunks from its bones. The kids watched in sober-minded awe, their lungs seeming to chug as one, heaving with the weight of the moment. They were all shell-shocked – shocked to be alive and shocked to have witnessed death.

Carson's brow was stuck in a permanent crease as his mind seemed to wrestle with the unknown. Of course, he didn't know anything. As far as he knew, every adult just suddenly morphed into a rotten, ravaging, flesh-eating zombie. Kylie, too, was shaking her head, the color of the flames' light reflecting in her gorgeous eyes, matching the fire that was usually inside them. Declan would often find himself staring at them. And he'd find her often staring back with fiery anger. It was still worth it.

"Thank you," Quinn said wearily.

Declan was about to say, "you're welcome," when he saw Quinn slap his hand down on Carson's shoulder.

Carson nodded solemnly. "No problem. You guys all okay?"

Declan was slack-jawed. He couldn't believe his brother.

"Declan, you alright?" Carson asked, noticing Declan's disgusted face. "It's okay. We'll get through this."

Declan was steaming. Unfiltered words formed in his mouth, but something tamped them down just in time. He'd seen too many zombie movies to fall into that trap. Disunity killed too many teams. Rivalry, jealousy, selfishness led too many hapless victims into the undead hordes through stupid mistakes or outright vengeance. Many times, other humans were more dangerous than the zombies. But he couldn't let that happen. He'd rise above those clichés in a second.

"I'm fine. How 'bout you, Quinn? Your leg have any bite marks in it?"

Quinn ignored him. "We have to find the lamb." He looked at his watch.

Declan glanced at the watch as well, puzzled. So it still worked? Ender had knocked out all electricity, and Declan's phone, but he'd spared Quinn's smart watch? That means Ender hadn't sent out some EMP or something. He had full control and had used it to spite Declan with a burning phone. *What a jerk.*

Quinn sighed. "We have five minutes until the next catastrophe."

Kylie arched her brow, confronting Quinn. "What are you talking about?"

Quinn held Ender up and opened his mouth to explain, but the discus-god had the first word. "Oh, goodie. More adolescent heroes to save the day. And you'll explain it all to them. Make sure not to leave the good parts out about how I have incredible power and how Declan is a moron."

Quinn blinked hard in frustration before starting from the beginning, trying to explain how a sarcastic bird bath had just spoken. Meanwhile, Declan continued watching outside, plans and priorities rushing to his mind. There were many things up in the air – like where Bo Peep and her lamb could be – but there were also several certainties.

One, they had to get out of there. Several zombies were ambling toward their home. Sure, the door was locked shut, but the windows weren't boarded up, and they didn't have time. Before long, one would fall straight through, inviting the others in to crash the party with loud moans. Two, they had to find weapons and survival gear. Sure, the world would end in less than an hour – but they had to survive a few more unknown catastrophes in that time.

Quinn was telling Carson and Kylie about the sacrifice when Declan turned to the kids they had rescued. They were holding onto Kylie's jacket, crying. They had to be no more than eight years old. Probably brother and sister. He leaned down to their level, speaking calmly. "Hey, kids."

They turned to him with watery eyes.

"Have you seen a girl dressed in a shepherdess costume?"

"Ally?" the girl asked in her small voice.

Declan rolled his eyes. "How the heck should I know her name? Wouldn't I have said her name instead of 'girl dressed in a shepherdess costume'? *Seriously.*"

The girl clung tighter to Kylie. The others gave him disapproving glares.

Declan tuned back his anger and cleared his throat. "Sorry. Where did you last see her – Ally…with the shepherdess costume?"

There was a deep quiet as they waited for her answer.

"She was running from one of those things."

BANG!

The group startled, swinging their necks toward the basement door.

"They're inside." Carson warned.

"Nah, it's just our mom," Declan said. "But the others…" he peered through the window at the lumbering figures silhouetted by the light of the flaming car," …will be here soon." Declan seized the silence. "So we have to get ready. This is the zombie apocalypse guys. We need weapons and gear, and we need them now!"

Declan met eyes with Quinn and then Carson. Neither boy responded. Maybe they were too in awe of his take-charge attitude that they couldn't move. Or, more likely, they were politely telling him that a taking-charge Declan was absurd.

Disappointed, Declan turned in a huff, marching through the kitchen

43

to the garage. He grabbed the keys to the Tahoe and pocketed them. He had made it to the garden tools when he heard the creak of steps behind him. When he turned, he saw the others standing in the doorway behind Carson.

"You know zombies, huh?" Carson asked.

Declan smiled.

In two minutes, the garage door began to open, revealing the group to the chaos outside. Quinn, still in his George Washington outfit, complete with body-length blue coat and white wig, wore a long-strapped duffel bag he had commandeered to hold the disc and wielded a long, vicious-looking garden scythe, its curving blade the thing of nightmares. The pirate, Trevor, was armed with his hook-for-a-hand and a brick that was tied to a length of rope wound around his body. Declan had thoroughly ridiculed him for the choice, but the kid was as stubborn as he was stupid.

Kylie had grabbed a hatchet in one hand and a trash can lid for a shield in the other. Carson's satchel was filled with ball bearings for slingshot ammo, a multi-tool, a lighter, a golf ball, and an assortment of other knickknacks he never knew might come in handy.

And then there was Declan, wearing a bicycle helmet and a gardener's belt. The belt held an armory of garden tools – a garden spade, a three-pronged weeding tool, and a garden shears. But his weapon of choice was the classic pitch fork. Just in case, he'd also stuffed his backpack full of fireworks.

Before the door was even halfway up, Declan was barking hushed instructions. "We have to stick together. Knock them down or knock their heads – nothing else works. And if you get bit, you better dang tell everyone."

The door clunked all the way open, the sounds of the apocalypse washing over them – the growls and animalistic howls of the zombies, the shrieks of their victims, and the pleas for help from those who were next. There was the smell of smoke and gas from the flaming wreck – or from some other fire in town – but there were no sirens or helicopters or any vehicles at all. The lights were still out, leaving the moon to paint the cacophony in blue hues.

"Which way did Ally run?" Carson asked the little girl who stayed latched to Kylie.

"That way," she said, pointing.

Carson nodded as they moved out with timid steps, Declan taking the point of a triangle formation. "Oh, not sure if they're drawn by sound, smell, or sight yet so keep it quiet."

They inched further out, their heads on swivels, watching the zombies within sight. There were three at the front of the house, a clown-costumed one punching down the window, the other two banging on the door. As quiet as they were, they weren't attracting any attention. So far so good.

"QUIET IS SO BO-OOORING!" Ender squawked.

All at once, the zombies stopped their manic assault on the front of the house and turned to the huddle of children. And the girl screamed.

Kylie snapped her hand over the girl's mouth, but it was useless. They had already been spotted, targeted, and salivated over.

Declan tensed. Every muscle went taut, as if he were cresting the peak of a rollercoaster. His knuckles went white on the pitchfork's handle as his mind raced toward paralysis. Could he actually do this? Could he actually ram a sharp object into another person? Or were these still people? Could they somehow be saved – or were their souls

45

already long gone?

The closest zombie waddled closer. He was an obese clown with tufts of orange hair, a bulbous red nose, and flakey white skin that fell from his face like dried paint. Declan gulped as he approached. He braced his feet, halting the formation and preparing for the lunge. The clown's feet hit the driveway. Its bulging fat shook like jelly.

Declan raised the pitchfork to his shoulder, took a deep breath.

The clown came within range. He could hear the moaning coming from its lungs. Its smell reached his nostrils.

Declan willed himself to do it, clenched his teeth, closed his eyes, and drove the pitchfork forward.

But it found nothing but air. Declan lost his balance and opened his eyes. The clown had fallen to the ground, a dark hole in its forehead. The other two zombies fell with similar deaths after two snaps of Carson's slingshot.

Declan gulped in air, relieved that it was over – at least for now – and that he had done it. Well, he had *tried* to do it at least. Again, Carson had stolen his glory, but it wasn't his fault. That's just who Carson was – always trying to save people, even if they didn't need saving.

"Watch right!" Carson chided from the back.

Declan swung around to see a small herd of the zombies coming from the alley between houses. It must have been a neighborhood Halloween party. There was a witch, a leather-clad cat-woman, a Wookie, an inflatable sumo-wrestler, and more, all moaning and groaning, with arms stretching toward their small huddle.

Declan looked for an escape but saw zombies converging on them from all sides. Maybe it was the car fire, or the moaning of the

46

curtained-zombie that was drawing them. Or maybe it was their smell. There was no way to know for sure, but it wasn't looking good.

"You guys are done for," piped Ender from Quinn's bag.

"Shut it!" Declan shouted, spinning to engage the zombie herd.

THUNK! The cat woman's head reeled back from a vicious impact, but all that Declan had seen was a red blur. But then the offending projectile fell to the driveway with a clunk, still tied to the rope that Trevor now used to reel it in. By the time the cat woman had fallen on her back, Trevor had the brick ready for another throw.

Declan shrugged, somewhat impressed, but reluctant to show it. Besides, the herd was still coming.

If Trevor can do it, so can I.

This time, without thinking, he thrust the pitch fork into the Wookie's head. Before the Wookie's weight could pull him down with the pitch fork, Declan yanked it free with a slurp, letting the Wookie fall to the ground at his feet. It would have sickened him to think about it, even for a second – but he didn't have a second. None of them did. The others were swinging and chopping and slinging, cutting into the herd left and right, and Declan heard more shuffling of feet to his left. Another one was coming.

It was a motorcyclist with a full-visored helmet, tight black jacket, and riding gloves, only ten feet from him. Declan swung his pitchfork, its sharp ends still black from the Wookie-zombie's blood, and jabbed it at the zombie's head. But the forks plinked off its helmet, and the zombie was two steps closer, bearing down on him with gloved hands.

Regaining his balance, Declan stepped back and thrust again in panic, sticking the forks into the creature's chest. Unaffected by pain, the creature kept its momentum through the fork, pressing further

47

toward Declan. Declan bent his knees and dug in, pushing back the beast with all his might. The beast staggered backwards and slipped off the forks, but it was rather agile for a zombie.

In a moment, it had regained its balance and come back full-steam into the pitchfork, letting it sink into its belly. Pressing forward, its hand reached for Declan's face, but Declan pushed it back again, only to have it come back again, making new punctures in its abdomen. The next time, though, Declan pushed and twisted. The undead motorcyclist slipped off the forks and tumbled on the grass.

Using the time it took for the zombie to get back to its feet, he turned to his friends to lend a hand. But it was just then that disaster struck. Kylie swung her hatchet into the inflatable sumo-wrestler's chest, but the thin plastic suit deflated and wrapped around her blade too easily, swallowing her momentum. She was down in a flash, the zombie then tripping over her and onto Trevor in a pile of writhing bodies.

Time seemed to slow down as adrenaline flooded his system. All at once he could see the former sumo-wrestler biting Trevor's fake parrot, Trevor's hook finding its way into the zombie's eye socket, and the goo gushing forth. Then with all the strength he had, Trevor was yanking the creature away like a hooked fish.

At the same time, a flash of movement whisked across the street. With a glance, Declan saw Little Bo Peep – Ally – riding a bike, pedaling hard to evade a determined zombie. Even in his desperation, he heard the lamb's frightened bleating.

If his heart would've beat faster, it probably would've popped. But he still felt a jolt of excitement in the midst of all the overwhelming fear. The lamb and its beautiful protector were alive. Their salvation. They could stop this chaos if they could only catch her!

And then something brought him down from behind.

The undead motorcyclist had grabbed his ankles, sending him tumbling back toward Trevor and knocking the two small children down on the way. Disoriented, he lost the pitch fork and his bearings. In the whirlwind there were limbs, more lumbering shapes of zombies bearing down, and weird streaks of fire in the sky.

But when he finally came to his senses, the zombie was biting at the girl's face.

Chapter 7

It was a good thing the zombie was wearing a full helmet, otherwise its bites would have actually torn into the girl's face. Instead, it merely rubbed its helmet hard against the girl's cheek and nose, smooshing it to the side.

Declan didn't wait to marvel at the weird sight. In between the girl's squeals, Declan reached over, raised the helmet's visor, and jabbed his garden shears inside as hard as he could. He felt the resistance and then a jerk before the zombie's body went limp.

He then turned over, facing Trevor on his stomach. The boy still held back the yawning, growling zombie with his hook digging into the creature's eye-socket. Black goo dribbled down like tears, saliva trailed from its rotten, jagged teeth, and its glazed eyes contained nothing but blood-lust and death. It was soulless, hungry, and inches from its meal. Declan aimed his shears for its temple and thrust.

Trevor pushed the body away, pulling his hook free with a sick slurp.

Scrambling to their feet, the group was back in formation in seconds, just in time for the end. Dozens of zombies were hemming them in, Ally had disappeared, and they were already exhausted. Zombie fighting wasn't as easy as the movies made it out to be. Sure, one movie had been correct in saying that one of the most important things in the zombie apocalypse was cardio. Declan's cardio was doing well — if doing well meant beating so hard it could win a heavy-weight boxing match.

"How much time until the next catastrophe?" Carson asked.

Quinn gave the stoic reply. "None."

Declan eyed the three closest zombies. A pitch-fork wouldn't hold them all off. If only his step-dad had owned a chainsaw...

"What do we do?" Quinn asked, backing closer to the group.

Even Carson was at a loss. "I...I..."

The trio of zombies growled and hissed, staggering closer and closer. Declan raised his pitchfork to the shoulder. If he was going down, he'd take at least one of them with him.

Then there was a deep *THRUM* from Quinn's bag.

WOOOSH!

A streak of red fire obliterated the zombies. Shrapnel from the street smacked Declan's face, and he reacted a moment later, turning away from the incredible noise and light. The shockwave of whatever it was that had streaked into the driveway hit him, knocked him backward, and took away his breath.

For a moment he couldn't see or breathe, but a few coughs and blinks brought him back to his senses. Still, a gray haze of evaporated asphalt filled the air. He hacked even as more streaks fell from sky to earth, erupting into plumes of dirt and fantastic blasts that ripped zombies to shreds.

The second catastrophe.

"How's that for timing?" Ender chirped. "You guys are seriously lucky..."

"Quick!" Carson cried. "Back to the garage!"

He didn't have to say it twice. The group hauled toward the open garage door, slicing at the zombies on the way and maneuvering around simmering craters with fireballs still smoking inside them. With each explosion, debris rained on their heads and heat radiated from the basketball-sized meteorites, so intense that Declan felt his arm hair begin to curl. Sweat dripped from his forehead and lip, both from heat and exertion. But they were almost back inside.

With one last thrust of the pitchfork into zombie chest, he left it behind, sticking the handle in the ground so that the zombie's momentum kept it pushing the handle deeper and deeper into the lawn.

He ran into the garage as another fireball smashed through the house, sending flames erupting through the windows in a shower of glass.

"Keys!" Carson yelled.

"I got 'em!" Declan replied, pushing past Carson to the driver's door. "And I'm driving!"

Carson made a face, but relented, rushing to the passenger's side. But Declan noticed he stopped at the door, looking into the collapsing house. The wall to the living room had been blown out, and flames licked at the couch inside. But that's not what he was looking at. It was a female zombie, taking slow steps toward them.

Carson had raised his slingshot, but halted with the band shaking with primed energy. Declan gripped the keys as they rested in the ignition, hesitating as he realized with Carson who it was. He was thankful that Carson had chosen to hold his fire. Maybe, somehow, she could be turned back. Maybe she could still mother him, nag him, and love him again someday.

"Get in!" he yelled as he turned the ignition. The engine rumbled to life, Carson jumped inside, and he hit the gas.

The SUV jolted forward and smashed into their freezer, knocking it straight through the garage's back wall and causing an avalanche of roof supports and shingles.

Declan slammed the brakes and made a wide-eyed, apologetic look at the passengers. Carson cocked his head, communicating with his eyes that he was ready to take the wheel if Declan couldn't handle it.

"I know, I know! Hold on!"

He jerked the gear shifter to Reverse and hit the gas again. This time they rocketed in the right direction. The remains of the roof clattered and screeched as they shed from the hood, rolling free. The passengers snapped their seat belts just in time; the vehicle rocked violently, its wheels seeming to find every piece of debris or zombie body as Declan piloted it around the fiery craters and into the road.

The destruction was fantastic. Houses erupted in shrapnel and flame in every direction. The road rippled like disturbed water. The whole city was churning, like a puddle assaulted with a bucket of pebbles. But these weren't pebbles. The smallest fireballs were like baseballs. The biggest were as big as the rock that chased Indiana Jones – as big as their car! And then Declan realized Carson was dressed as Indy. *How appropriate.*

A meteor crashed to their right and bounced over their hood, inches from their windshield. It proceeded to destroy a line of cars parked on the street. Declan watched it and forgot to keep his eyes on the road. In a small miracle, he turned back just in time to swerve around a neighbor's house – but not the garden...the bushes...or the fence.

Smack after smack, they careened through the yard and finally back onto a road.

"Declan..." Carson began.

"SHH!" he responded, peering forward with steely eyes.

"That's right," came Ender's voice from the bag. "Declan needs focus. Only think one thing at time. Declan drive bad."

Quinn took the disc from the bag, holding it for Kylie and the kids to see. Declan couldn't afford to take his eyes off the road for one second, though, as he spun the wheel, squealing the tires as he centered the SUV in the direction he had last seen Ally. More meteors came streaking down like golf balls at a popular driving range. And they were the hole.

Dirt and sod hit their windshield, and the wipers only helped so much. He stretched his neck, finding a good view as he pushed down on the accelerator and barreled forward.

"She went this way? Why would she go this way?" he asked, hoping the kids would have an answer.

The girl shrugged. "I don't know. The school?"

Declan nodded, knuckles white on the steering wheel as they zigged and zagged through the neighborhood.

THUD!

A zombie dressed as…a zombie…complete with make-up and torn clothes, disappeared under their grill. Declan smiled to himself at the irony. A little comic relief eased his tension.

"Hey, you!" Kylie exclaimed.

Declan glanced in the rear-view mirror as Kylie yelled at Ender, who was being inspected by Quinn.

"My name is DOOM! Ender of Worlds!"

"Okay, Doom – whatever," Kylie responded. "We get this lamb for you, and you stop all this, right?"

Ender sighed. "I don't answer questions."

"At least tell us if we're on the right track," Kylie pleaded. "Help us out here."

"No way. Not helping at all. Just watching. And so far it's quite entertaining, but it's not really believable yet. I think once a character dies, then I'll get really invested, you know. I'll get the feels."

She scowled, continuing to search the windows for Ally.

Quinn shrugged at Kylie then examined the disc again. "The next picture is three wavy lines. Like it's wind or water."

"Or air condithioning," Trevor added.

"Or snakes," the boy suggested.

Carson shuddered. "*Anything* but snakes."

Declan piloted the SUV into a mailbox before zipping over a curb, onto a street, and over another curb, jostling the passengers with neck-whipping turbulence.

Once they had settled, Carson slid open the sun roof, staring into the meteor-ridden night sky. Declan and the others gazed out with him, gaping at the awe-inspiring beauty. The flames were brilliant in light and scope. Thousands of shooting stars, racing toward the earth, miles away or just feet away in a massive wave of rock and fire. In the midst of the streaking flames was a dark shape floating across the tree line. It appeared to be a small UFO with a caged animal on top. Declan's brow furrowed in confusion, but he could only shake his head. There were weirder things than even that going on.

When he glanced back down, he saw an even greater surprise. "There!"

To their right was Bo Peep on her bike, riding through the cemetery on a winding sidewalk that meandered through the grave stones. The little lamb watched out the back of the basket, its two front hooves folded over the top.

"She's taking a shortcut to the school!" Quinn noted.

Declan yanked on the wheel to follow, churning toward the rickety, black gate.

"Roll down the window!" Kylie piped. "Tell her to stop!"

Declan heard Carson lower the windows just before they rammed through the massive gate that flew off its hinges. Once he'd cleared the gate, he turned the SUV to straddle the sidewalk, tearing up the manicured grass on either side. Flames from the streaking fireballs cast an eerie light to the hills of gravestones and smoke clouds drifting in from nearby fires. The flickering light, smoke, and graves made for one horribly creepy atmosphere.

Ally was only fifty yards away now, but she swung her head around, catching a glimpse of them careening toward her. She was frightened even more, taking a drastic turn from the sidewalk into the graves.

It was then that Declan noticed the hands.

They were rising from the graves, digging, plunging upward, desperate to free themselves from their rotten coffins. Dozens of them had broken surface, reaching into the air. Some grabbed at the girl's tires. She screamed, nearly toppling as she lost her balance.

Anger burned in his chest. Stupid zombies would not take her. He'd only just met her. They needed more time. The universe owed it to him. And their connection was real. Undeniable. He already had the protective instinct of a jealous boyfriend. And it felt good somehow. It felt right.

Declan stepped harder on the accelerator.

THUD! THUD THUD!

Those hands stopped reaching. No one would touch her. Especially not dead people.

"Ally!" Carson called out from the window. "ALLY! STOP!"

But Declan knew it was hopeless. The meteors were whining,

sizzling, slamming the ground in a great, endless cacophony. She wouldn't be able to hear them until they were practically next to her.

CRUNCH! Declan piloted them over a headstone.

"Fine, Ender. Don't answer questions. Just tell us what you think we should do," Quinn said, with a hint of *aren't-I-clever* in his eyes.

Ender sighed long and hard. "Look. I know I said I wouldn't help..."

The kids sucked in air, hope rising in their hearts for any kind of a clue.

"...so I won't help. I'm a disc of my word."

"You're horrible," Kylie moaned.

"I know, I know. I'm so evil, despicable, handsome...I've heard it all before. But your group is literally the stupidest group of morons I've ever seen. Monkeys could do better. I mean, who drives through a cemetery in the zombie apocalypse?"

"Aha!" Quinn blurted. "You hear that, guys? Chasing after this lamb isn't smart. That's what he's saying. We're on the wrong trail."

"Talking about the wrong trail...," Declan was already leaning over the wheel and squinting into the thickening smoke, "...I think we lost her."

He slowed the vehicle to a crawl, hunched over the wheel, peering into the smoke blanket that lingered over the grassy hills in thick clouds, churning inward and washing over their hood. The headlights were useless now, only illuminating the whirls of smoke and the zombies' faces as they latched – "Aagh!"

Zombies!

Declan hit the accelerator again, churning up grass and banging through gravestone as the fireballs continued pelting the earth around them. Trevor screamed and Carson gripped the dashboard as Declan

57

veered left and right, shaking off the herd of latching zombies like rag dolls.

"Get out of here!" Carson yelled.

"Yeah! We need shelter! Still three minutes of this!" Quinn announced with a girlish shriek to his voice.

With no time to respond, Declan punched through the opposite gate, sending it sparking along the street and into a crater. With a too-sudden yank of the wheel, he whipped them around with a squeal, the g-force stiffening his neck with protruding veins. Finally, he straightened them out, free of zombies and unharmed by any fireballs. The SUV rocked to a stop, giving the kids a moment to recollect their thoughts.

"We have to find her!" Carson said first. "Maybe her lamb will work or maybe not – but she still needs our help."

Declan took in a deep breath and nodded his agreement, despite a nagging part of him that wanted Carson to keep his chick-magnet heroics to himself on this one. "Right. And it's only a matter of time before she gets hit with…"

BANG!

Chapter 8

Declan hadn't seen it coming. He didn't even know what had happened until later. But in an instant, their engine had gone from a powerful, intricate machine to a metal pancake. The impact had sent the rest of the vehicle into the air and back down with a jarring crash and an ear-rattling metal shriek. When he had opened his eyes again, the cracked windshield obscured much of the destruction. But it didn't cover up the heat of the flames and the pungent smell of smoke.

The passengers groaned and rubbed their aching necks and backs, the reality of the situation suddenly sinking in.

"Get out," Quinn groaned from the back. "The fire. Gas tank...!"

Carson was the first out, wielding the slingshot on the closest zombie and pushing one of the ones that had latched onto their hood back to the ground with a well-placed kick.

Declan stumbled out, staring at the stub-nosed vehicle in dismay. His step-dad would be peeved. But then he realized that his step-dad may actually never come home to discover that it was missing. He was probably staggering around the bar like usual, but this time for eternity.

Another meteor impact shook him from his reverie, and he jumped to action, helping the two kids from the vehicle.

Thankfully, the smoke was clearing with a change in wind. It wisped to the south, away from the street and back into the cemetery, where more and more zombies were unearthing themselves with howls of joy that sounded like broken tornado sirens of doom and misery.

"There!" Quinn shouted, pointing down the street.

The girl had been right. Ally was heading to the school for some reason. Unfortunately, she was a little late to the game. Fireballs had been smashing into the school for eight minutes now, putting pock holes in the roof, blasting out its windows, and setting its welcome sign on fire. It read, "Have a safe and happy Halloween" in melting black letters.

A huge smile spread on Declan's face. "School's out for…*ever*."

"Cool," said the boy, who, as far as Declan knew, didn't have a name.

Declan held a fist toward Boy, and Boy pounded it with his knuckles.

"I can't hold them off forever!" Carson shouted from the rear, zipping ball bearings into zombie skulls.

Again, snapping back to reality, Declan wielded his garden spade and prepared to enter the battle. But he stopped, nearly taking a scythe blade to the face as Quinn cocked back for a heavy swing that decapitated a near-skeletonized zombie fresh from the cemetery.

"Holy geez!" Declan exclaimed, exchanging a look of mutual amazement with Quinn.

Suddenly Declan's spade felt very inadequate. Instead, he raced to the smoldering truck and retrieved his backpack full of fireworks. Maybe a couple rockets to the eye socket would take them out.

He was closing the warped door when he heard it. A baby's cry. Such an odd sound in an apocalypse. He opened and closed the door again to make sure it wasn't making a baby-crying sound. *Nope.* There was definitely a crying baby somewhere. Even amid raining fire, crushing impacts, and groaning zombies, there it was. And it wasn't just a "I'm hungry" type of cry, this was the scared, grating chalkboard-type cry that sent chills down Declan's spine. His mind ran to horrible images of what zombies would do to a little baby.

60

He couldn't let that happen.

He found himself running toward the sound; then, once he reached the last house before the school's parking lot, he noticed that Kylie was right behind him. Together they chugged through the door, weapons raised.

But they stopped immediately.

What they saw boggled their minds.

A female zombie was carrying her baby with one of those baby-carrier backpacks. There was the mother, rotting and ravenous, spinning in circles, trying to catch and eat the baby strapped to her back. It was like a dog chasing its own tail – but with seriously scary consequences. The cute baby was wearing a headband with bunny ears but was bawling her eyes out.

It was a surreal moment, and they couldn't stop looking. How long had the mother been twirling? Almost twenty minutes? Would it continue to be this way until the baby died of starvation? How many other babies out in the world were encountering worse? The realization hit hard – but not as hard as Kylie's hatchet hit the woman.

"Catch her!" Kylie said as she swung.

Declan understood just in time, lunging out and catching the zombie's body as it fell to the ground with a hatchet in its skull. Then, with a mother's ferocity, Kylie unstrapped the baby and pulled it into her loving grasp. Still with one free hand, she tugged the hatchet free, wiped it on her equestrian pants, and sheathed it.

Declan was in awe. The dangerous kind of awe that occupied one's every thought. He didn't realize he was staring until she gave him that fiery stare of hers. "Get the carrier off her. I'll need it."

"Oh," he said after a few seconds of slow-turning gears. "Sure."

He found the snapping mechanism and pulled it free.

"Okay. Put it on me. Hurry." She turned around, singing and whispering and rocking the baby.

When Declan held the carrier up, it appeared to be a mess of straps and snaps and loops.

"Hurry," she repeated. Then she looked back to see him raising one strap after another with confusion. With a huff she pointed at the thickest band. "That's the belt, Doofus."

"Oh," he repeated, holding the belt. And then he looked down to where he was supposed to put it. Suddenly a lump rose in his throat and his hands shook more than when they had been when driving through a cemetery of cannibalistic monsters.

With those same trembling hands, he reached around her waist. As he peaked around her to guide the snap in, he saw Carson gaping at them from the doorway, the rest of the crew right behind. And behind them was another crew of the undead.

Carson's eyes met Declan's and sent daggers slicing into his pupils. Declan gulped down the hard lump in his esophagus. Carson and Kylie weren't exactly officially a couple, but imposing on whatever they had together would be a solid notch in his stupidity belt, right below the one he had gotten for calling Carson's mom a babe. And this notch should actually be two. A part of him felt guilty for even thinking about Kylie when Ally was lost and alone. Sure, he'd only known her for thirty seconds, but still. That had been a solid half-minute!

Click! The belt snapped in and Declan backed away with hands surrendered in the air.

Though Carson was clearly thinking of revenge, he said nothing, instead ushering everyone inside and slamming the door in the faces of several vicious zombies. Their pounding fists and raspy growls played through the door as it rattled in its frame.

Kylie was busy strapping the baby in the carrier, but the others were still on a mission. They raced past Declan to the back patio, where the school was just a hundred yards away across a parking lot that was completely barren – apart from the few spaces occupied by red-hot balls of fire.

Across the smoking expanse, a white bicycle was parked by the school's front doors.

"Alright," Carson began while pacing, "She's in the school. Quinn, how much time we got?"

Quinn peeked at his watch. "One minute."

Boy added, "Until the snakes." Then he gave a mischievous grin.

Declan held out a congratulatory fist to the boy and received a bump.

Carson gave a quick eye roll. "Whatever it is, it'll mean we're half an hour from the end of the world. You guys stay here, batten down the hatches, and figure out what to do. I'll get Ally and the lamb and bring them back."

An eruption of objections flooded Carson's way but Declan's was louder than the rest. "Heck, no! In every zombie movie, when they split up, they die. It just happens. We have to stick together. *I'll* go get her."

Quinn gave his brother a confused look, holding his scythe in one hand and a backpack strap in the other. "Carson's right. We have to split up. We don't have much time, and what if we don't find that lamb? What if a lamb's not even the right thing? Some of us have to try the lamb, the others need to stay and keep Ender safe."

"Why, thank you!" Ender exclaimed. "But I'm not the one in need of protecting. In twenty-eight seconds, things might start getting bad. For you."

Carson put his hand on the sliding glass door. "That's it. I'm going."

"Wait," Quinn said. "You both go." He looked at Declan. "That way if one of you doesn't make it, the other can let us know."

Declan gave him a long, concerned look. His brother was cold. Not like *brr* cold, but like *heart-of-ice* cold. He was willing to use his brother and friend as pawns in the apocalyptic game of chess. Though Declan had never played chess, he understood that pawns died first, sacrificing themselves for the good of the team. It just irked him that Quinn was the one with his fingers on the pieces.

"Fine. He can come with me," Declan concluded, nodding at Carson. Then he turned back to Quinn. "You keep Kylie safe."

Kylie scowled at him, but it didn't last long. She looked around, as if something had changed. And it had.

Only after a few seconds did they realize that the fireballs had stopped thumping the earth. After ten minutes of a constant bombardment, the sound had faded to the background in their minds. But now, when it was gone, the world seemed almost too quiet. There were the zombies still banging the doors and a crackling of fires, but that seemed like nothing compared to what had been. They awaited the next big catastrophe, but none came. At least not right away.

"It's settled," Carson said defiantly. "And please just try to freaking remember *exactly* what Ender said. If the lamb doesn't work, we need a plan B." With that, he slid open the door and raced toward the parking lot.

Declan *wanted* to stay. Staying was safer and Kylie was here. He caught eyes with Kylie, who now had her arms wrapped around Boy

64

and Girl, with Baby strapped on her back. Her eyes said it all. She was staying to protect them.

Ally was hot and provided cake and all, but Kylie was Kylie. She had always been his hidden crush, and the whole end of the world thing was just confirming his feelings for her.

Maybe she inspired him to go out and protect Ally, protect Carson and that stupid lamb. Or maybe he just wanted to save Ally and reap the hug in reward.

Either way, he had to go headfirst into the coming catastrophe.

"I'll be baa-aaack," he said with a sheep's voice.

The others stared at him. Boy chuckled.

Then, with that, he raced after Carson. When he looked back, Trevor was right behind, joining him on a whim. And Quinn was locking the door behind them.

Chapter 9

Declan's feet pounded the pavement, trying desperately to follow Carson's mad sprint toward the white bike. There was no chance he'd keep up, of course, but the slower he went, the farther he was from Carson's protective slingshot. And it was also good to put distance between him and Trevor, who was lagging even farther behind. The farther he got from Trevor, the greater the chance that zombies or the coming flood of snakes would get to him first. At least, in theory.

But of course, he was wrong. There was no flood of snakes. And the flood that came didn't come from behind. It came from everywhere.

They heard Ender's *THRUM* resound, even here.

And Carson was the first to see what it was. His feet shuffled to a stop near a crater, kicking debris down its side. Declan caught up to him and joined his gaze at the meteorite that still glowed red, like a simmering piece of coal. He didn't see anything that stuck out as weird (besides the normal weirdness of a meteorite in the school parking lot). But he *did* hear it.

"Whatth wrong?" Trevor asked, lumbering into them from behind.

"Shh!" Declan hushed, putting his hands on his knees to get closer to the sound, though his jagged breaths betrayed him.

Then they listened, all three of them pointing their ears toward it.

It was a low hissing sound with distinct crackling. They'd all heard it before but couldn't place it.

"Snakes?" Declan asked, leaning closer.

Carson took a noticeable step back, but Trevor leaned closer, nearly pushing Declan inside. A glare made the cross-eyed boy back off.

66

"No," Carson said, more resolved than afraid. "Something else. It's sizzling."

Then the answer came gushing forth, in a hot spray of steam.

HISSSS!

When Declan managed a glance into the crater despite the boiling hot steam rising in great gusts, he didn't see snakes. He saw water. Gurgling, churning from the earth like lava about to erupt.

"It's a flood," Carson said, his eyes already searching for a plan, darting from the bicycle back to the crater that was already nearly full. Maybe he was calculating the rate of the water's rise and the distance to the girl, trying to figure out if they had time to rescue her.

Declan was calculating as well – not so much with actual math – but with his gut. And his gut was telling him what to do with no uncertainties.

When the water rushed over the edge of the crater – and the other dozens of craters dotting the parking lot – both Carson and Declan had their answer.

They spoke simultaneously. "Let's go!"

But they took their first steps in opposite directions. Now they stood staring at each other, the water from all the craters already colliding to form a giant quarter-inch pool the size of a football field.

"I'm going for her. Do what you want!" Carson declared.

"No, wait!" Declan yelled, halting Carson's progress for a fraction of a second. In that time, Declan second-guessed himself. Who was he to challenge Carson? He was like the best kid he knew. He got straight A's at school, was athletic, and just plain good. And here Declan was, one of the weakest, most morally questionable, buck-toothed wannabe-heroes challenging him. Who did he think he was? But then again, Carson deserved to know what Declan was thinking.

"We don't know how high it's going to get," Declan said with an embarrassing whiny tone. "If you find her...where will you go?"

A crash of thunder forced them to pause.

Carson looked torn. "I...I don't know. Got a better plan?"

The water was already engulfing their shoes. Trevor was stomping in it as if it were a giant puddle.

"A boat," Declan said, matter-of-factly. "And I happen to know where one is."

He pointed toward the wooden fence separating a row of houses from the parking lot. Just over the crest of the fence was a lump of tarp covering something that Declan knew to be a boat. It was nothing special – but it had served as a convenient make-out hideaway for many a rowdy couple. Declan may or may not have had many opportunities to try it out, but he didn't like to kiss-and-tell.

"It's called the Lip Dock, or the S.S. Recess, one of the best locations for..."

"Doesn't matter!" Carson yelled, darting toward the school. He turned back, still at a run. "Get it and meet at the roof! Go!"

And with that, Carson was off, splashing toward the bicycle that had water lapping at its pedals. Declan sighed with an extra weight in his lungs. He already felt the impending failure nipping at his pride, even before he had tried. But he didn't have long to linger in self-pity. Another deep lungful of air and a barrage of sudden rain made a shiver of urgency run up the length of his arms. With a nod to himself, he straightened his James Bond tie, slapped a brother-in-arms type of hand on Trevor's already soaked shoulder, then burst toward the fence.

68

Chapter 10

Declan reached the fence and jumped for the top ledge but came away only with splintered fingers. Picking a splinter out of his thumb, he had just concluded that they would need to go around when Trevor came running over with his characteristic waddle, made more pronounced as he kicked at the shin-deep water.

"Me firtht!" Trevor shouted.

Declan scoffed. "Do you know how to unload a boat?"

"No. But I have thith." He held up the dangling brick, shining wet because of the pouring rain.

Declan sneered, dumbfounded and annoyed as rainwater dripped over his helmet's front like an overflowing gutter. "So...?"

"Puth me over and I'll throw the brick back over – then I'll pull you up. Or we can wait to thwim over if you'd rather."

After too long of a pause, Declan surrendered to the boy's logic and the rising tide. The kid was right. Somehow. "Whatever." He knelt and held out both hands, palms up.

In a jiffy the boy was up and over. Sure, Declan had given him an extra little push to get him over the peak, but there was water to soften the blow on the other side. He heard Trevor's squeal right before the deep splash.

"You alright?" he asked. *Don't care...* he muttered under his breath.

"Yup!" came Trevor's chipper reply as the brick flew over the fence with a rope for a tail. Then it reached the end of the rope and pendulumed toward Declan's face.

He dodged as the brick hit the fence with a loud thud.

"Geez!" he exclaimed, pulling the brick down sharply, hoping to give Trevor rope-burn. "Sure you can hold me?"

"How much do you weigh?" Trevor asked.

"Pre or post dump?"

"Whatever you are now."

"112 pounds."

"Really? You ate all our candy, didn't you?"

"Shut up. I'm getting on."

"Even the little candy pumpkinth?"

Ignoring the question, Declan grabbed high on the rope and jumped, lifting both feet to the brick. It was an awkward, twisting landing, but surprisingly, he was on with both feet, straddling the slippery rope and hanging on for dear life.

"Pull me up!"

He heard the grunting on the other side of the fence paired with splashing and a new sound. A concerning sound. Though it could have been Trevor's raspy grunts and wheezes, it was too deep – too angry.

These were the sounds zombies made when they were coming in for the kill.

Declan felt the brick raise him along the fence. His helmeted head was nearly to the top, but his hands were gripped so tightly to the rope he couldn't imagine letting go.

But the growls and moans were getting closer.

Suddenly he wasn't so sure about going over.

"Wait!" he yelled. "Is it safe?"

Trevor's reply was a mighty grunt that brought Declan up another few inches, just enough to give him the ability to pull himself over. But he stopped halfway over, nearly impaling his soft belly on the sharp fence posts.

As the posts dug in, he surveyed the scene. Sure enough, water was filling the backyard, wrapping around the house, forming a white-water rapids. Trevor was in the thick of it, being knocked around by the current, but he wasn't alone. There were other bodies rushing in, banging against the shed, the swing set, the fence. Their arms were flailing, reaching for Trevor, but they were too rigid and clumsy to affect their angles. They were victims of the current, barely keeping their heads above water.

But Declan knew they didn't need to be above the water to bite. His mind battled through fears.

Zombies in the water! Unseen gnashing teeth, snapping at his ankles, pulling him down deep, tearing into him.

He wanted to turn back. He tried. But the fence was stabbing him, and his balance was failing. His body tipped toward the water like a broken teeter-totter.

He hit the water in a back-flop and tumbled out of control.

GURGLE! GURGLE! GASP!

He broke through the top of the water and found his footing in the yard below. The frost-cold current was rushing against his waist, pushing him back into the fence, but he resisted it enough to stand and swipe his bangs from his eyes.

Adrenaline rushed through his exhilarated veins like the flood, his eyes racing to find the danger. The zombies. Where were they?

He scanned right to the swing set. There was one, tangled in the swing's ropes. There was something else – like a shark's fin just under the surface ahead. Ignoring it, he swung left to the boat with its name emblazoned on the side – the *S.S. Kerplunk*. It was still attached to the trailer. He could see the transom straps. Two of them held its stern to the trailer and a winch hook secured the boat's bow. He'd need to free all three. And then they'd need the keys.

Trevor had one eye on him, the other, lazy one was drifting toward the fin. He stuck his hooked hand in the water. "Here fishy-fishy!"

Declan caught his attention. "Trevor! Find the boat key! It's gotta be inside somewhere!"

Trevor managed to lock both eyes on him for a moment before the other rolled away to who knows where. He saluted Quinn. "Aye aye matey!" Then he chugged against the water, heading to the sliding glass doors.

The water was now at Declan's abdomen. He turned to the boat and hopped toward it with feeble paddles. It was slow-going, but swimming with a backpack full of fireworks, shoes, and a suit would not be any faster. Before long, though, he would be without an option. When he finally approached the boat, the water was at his ribs.

He snuck a glance back as he took off his backpack. Another zombie was carried into the yard, smacking into the fence. The fence shuddered and cracked, bowing out with the weight. The fin, though, was nowhere to be seen. Somehow that was of no comfort.

Shrugging it off, he undraped the tarp, heaved his backpack up and into the boat, and went to work on the first strap. He yanked on the handle, giving it slack just as a crashing sound startled him. It had been the sliding glass doors. He only got a quick glance before he was swept off his feet.

In his glance he had seen Trevor holding a length of rope trailing into the broken glass doors. In the next instant the water gushed inside the house, taking the boy with it.

72

It also took Declan. And the zombies.

He had tried to hold on to the strap, but the rush had been too fast and too strong. The current pulled him into the deep with no time to take a breath. He was underwater, eyes wide open, trying to make sense of his direction as the current carried him toward the house like a rag doll.

His body banged into something solid and then into something soft. When he pushed it away, he let out a scream with all the oxygen he had left. It was a shark, with a gaping mouth full of white, triangular teeth. Where the neck should have been, there was a horribly disfigured zombie face with its own teeth and sickly brown eyes.

Then it was gone.

Declan's feet hit something hard, and he pushed at it, slowing his tumble just enough to reach out and grab at a wall. His fingers found grip. His eyes found a railing. A stairway. He was already inside the house. With a lunge, he snagged the railing and pulled himself against the current, finally finding relief from the rushing current at the foot of the stairs. Frantically, he gasped at air and crawled up two, three more steps until he was out of the water.

Still the water was rising another step every few seconds. He kept crawling and coughing until, finally, he had outpaced it. The volume of rushing water rescinded as the level inside the house matched that of the outside.

His mind raced. Where was Trevor? Was he okay? What about the boat? Could he get back to it? Should he find the keys first? Even so, could he make it to Carson in time – or to Kylie and Quinn? And what was that zombie-shark? Was that a part of another new catastrophe?

"Trevor? Trevor?!"

No answer.

But the fin was there. Cutting, slithering through the water, coming to the foot of the steps.

Declan's heart raced even faster. He backed up another step, his eyes plastered on the fin as it finally emerged from the water.

The figure that emerged was hulking, dark gray, dripping water, and walking.

Walking.

It rose to its full height, and its gaping cloth jaws exposed the zombie's human face inside. It rasped a growl. Chomped. Took another step up.

Costume or not, it was the most frightening thing he'd ever seen.

"Uh…nope," he muttered to himself. Then he swung around, shed his sodden shoes and suit-jacket, raced up the remaining stairs, and darted to the bedroom window overlooking the backyard.

And there it was. The water was nearly to the top of the boat. If the boat flooded, he'd never be able to bail it out on his own. He had to get down there and free it from the straps. And he had to do it now.

He took a nearby lamp, smashed it through the window, and backed up. He heard the zombie-shark growling behind him, but it didn't matter. With a deep breath, he took off and leapt through the open window.

Chapter 11

He hit the water in a near-perfect shallow dive and straightened out, zipping through the debris-filled water like he'd done it a hundred times.

The thing was, he had. His family – before the divorce – had been regular lake-goers. They'd spent hours diving, swimming, fishing, jet-skiing. He had docked and undocked boats, made friends with ladies at the marina, and searched for sunken treasures with not-entirely-certified SCUBA gear. To say the least, he was comfortable in the water.

But then again, this was different. The water, fresh from the bowels of the earth, was littered with debris that could have come from blocks away – from inside of houses or from the bottoms of lakes. There was clothing whisking by, a floating painting of a sailboat being struck by lightning, and everything from cereal boxes to shoes to cribs submerged and tumbling. And then there were the human shapes. Some weren't moving. Some were.

He didn't have time to deal with them. He emerged, spitting water and re-adjusting his bicycle helmet before his hands finished the first strap and nimbly bounced to the other.

As soon as he unlatched the second strap, the boat creaked and rose with the water. But it wasn't entirely free yet. The stern swung free, but the bow was still hung up on the leash of the winch hook. He'd have to get to the winch hook to free it.

He dove back in, breast-stroking through the dark water, brushing away ghostly sweaters and blankets that floated and bobbed like jellyfish. They weren't dangerous, but they did obscure his vision. He was only underwater for a few seconds, but that was all it took. He hadn't even seen it stalking him.

He pushed away a piece of clothing, revealing the shark's menacing eye! He nearly gulped in water with a gasp as the zombie-shark grabbed his arm and yanked it toward its open mouths – both its costumed mouth and its very real and deadly one.

But Declan's other hand was there just in time, grabbing the shark's costume and giving it a counter-push, keeping its jaws just inches from his other arm. Then he twisted and kicked, yelling silently and headbutting it with his helmet until he finally wrenched free.

Still, the zombie was relentless, breathing in water without a care. It grabbed at him, raked at his limbs, keeping him submerged. Declan fought, tearing away its grasps but always one move behind. And then he knew. He was going to drown like this. The starry light from above was getting farther away as the water rose, taking them both deeper and his lungs farther from air.

He felt pangs of pain in his chest. Panic began to cloud his vision. He tried to swim up and away, but the shark grabbed his leg. It was so strong! Too strong!

His energy was fading. He could feel it ebb. But he had to free himself. He had to!

He kicked and kicked. Something rubbed against his thigh. Then he recalled. He had the tool belt on his waist with one remaining tool.

With a flash of energy, he grabbed the hand rake and scraped its three sharp prongs along the zombie-shark's hand. Though it didn't feel pain, it couldn't hold onto his foot without tendons or muscles in its hand. He raked the hand two more times. Skin and dark goo floated free. He felt the prongs scrape on bones…and then he was free.

With a desperate last kick, he rocketed to the surface and gasped in a massive breath. The oxygen rushed to his brain. He took in deep swaths of air, nearly getting too dizzy to orient himself. The deluge of rain and the darkness didn't help. With only distant fires and moonlight to light the area, he felt lost, even in a backyard.

He spun, treading water, until he found the boat's outline. To his surprise, Trevor was in it. Waving.

"Trevor?"

"Hey! I got the keyth!" He held up the keychain. "Get on!" He threw out the brick as if it were a life preserver, shoved the keys in the ignition, and cranked the engine.

"Wait!" Declan yelled, but his voice was overpowered.

The motored propeller in back choked and sputtered, coughing as it churned to life under the water.

A part of Declan was ecstatic. *It worked!* Who knows how long the boat had been sitting out, unused. It was a small miracle it started so easily. The other, smarter part of Declan was not happy. This part of Declan knew that the winch hook was still connected. The boat wouldn't go anywhere but sideways, like a rabies-mad dog on a short leash.

Was he dizzy, or was the boat already spinning toward him? *Fast…*

He yelped and dove under as the boat's wild underside slid over him, knocking his helmet and back with a painful scrape. Again he was submerged with little breath, alone with the zombie-shark and a bladed propeller just asking to chop his limbs off. The engine's roar was muffled, but everything was a muffled gurgle in his ears. Still, he heard a cranking of metal on metal that signaled his fears had come true.

The water was raising the back of the boat; the propeller was kicking it around, but the front was still hooked to the trailer by the winch. If he didn't unhook it soon, Trevor would be toppled out and the boat submerged as the stern rose straight above the bow. And with that spinning propeller of death on the loose, Declan's body would probably become a pulpy mess of blood and flesh the zombie shark could drink with a straw.

Even as he thought this, he was instinctively kicking his legs and pumping his arms, swimming deeper than the propeller's blades could cut. He felt the water slashing above him as he descended just out of its reach.

Remembering the shark, he swung right and left, peering through loose shirts, a lampshade, and other debris, searching for the creature.

He didn't have to search long. It was behind the lampshade, its shark-suit just buoyant enough to keep it from sinking to the bottom, where several other zombies were drift-walking in slow-motion, lumbering steps. The zombie shark didn't appear to know how to swim, but its movements were somehow getting it closer and closer to him. Maybe it was the reaching, lunging movements, or maybe it was just the current. Either way, it was coming for him.

There was no way Declan was letting it sneak up on him again.

It was time to end him.

He slipped off his belt, swam up to the creature, and jammed the leather strap into its biting mouth. Then, pulling it into a backward roll, he aimed upward, toward the careening boat. Even as the creature clawed at his arms and bit at the leather strap, Declan smiled. Then he kicked with both legs, sending the creature upward, into the propeller's path. He watched it and cringed.

78

Chapter 12

Declan didn't have long to admire his work. He was nearly out of air and out of time. He surfaced in a safe area, motioned for Trevor to turn off the engine, and then swam to the hook. The boat's stern was a full three feet above the bow when he released the hook. The bow jerked free and shot upward. He had a brief regret for not warning Trevor about the possibility of whiplash – but that was short-lived.

Finally, after the long ordeal, he emerged at the boat's ladder and climbed aboard. Sure enough, Trevor was down and woozy from the boat's rocking, but Declan just stepped over him. He threw himself into the pilot's seat, restarted the engine, pushed the throttle up, and guided the craft through the alley between houses – and to relative safety.

As he piloted the boat by the second story windows, finally sitting after what had seemed like a non-stop parade of horrors, a seeming quiet descended on him. The panic could finally ebb, the adrenaline fade, and his thoughts expand to the new reality. He was soaked head to toe, water dripping from his bangs and chin; he blinked hard. He took in slower and slower breaths as he guided the boat onto the river that once was a suburban street. The reality finally began to sink in.

The flood had filled the entire town. What had once been a quiet mid-western town was now a lake of smoky ruins rising like lily pads in a giant pond. As far as the eye could see, there were only roofs, light poles, utility towers, and a lone water tower. Smoke hung in the air, thick and high, and a few roofs were still on fire despite the heavy rain. Through a gap in the smoke, the odd drone with a caged rodent hovered above. Declan didn't know how it still flew, but he knew it would run out of power eventually and have nowhere to go but the bottom of the deep.

Even as the water continued to lap at the boat, lifting it higher every second, Declan felt the cleansing power of the flood. It had put out fires, washed away the zombies, and was now hiding the broken town. Soon it would only be an ocean glowing in the moonlight. And the S.S. Kerplunk would be the only thing floating. Hopefully he and Trevor wouldn't be the only two alive.

"Here! Over here!" distant voices rang out.

Declan's heart lifted, and he swirled the boat toward the survivors' roof. Before long he swung the port side against the roof's peak. Trevor, now alert, threw his brick to Quinn as if it were an anchoring line. Quinn held it taut as the others piled in the boat, first the kids, and then Kylie with the baby. Declan caught Quinn's eyes as he waited for his turn. He hoped for some sort of recognition – some sort of congratulations or something – but all he got was a barrage of questions.

"Where's Carson? Did he find the lamb and…uh…Ally?"

"First of all, you're welcome. Second of all, shut up and get on. We have to get to the school."

Quinn knelt and dropped into the now-crowded boat, searching the dark horizon for the school. Declan knew what he was thinking. He himself had been thinking it, too. Most of the school was only one story tall. The gym and cafeteria were two stories tall, but those would be underwater in a matter of seconds. It wasn't looking good for Carson or Ally.

"Go, go!" Quinn commanded, suddenly in command again.

Declan arched his aching back and massaged his ego even as he hit the throttle again, squinting into the blistering rain. Maneuvering around debris, he managed one look behind as their wake rippled over the disappearing roof.

He turned back and focused on his navigation.

"Thanks, Declan."

Declan glanced to his side where Boy was standing, holding on to the side of the boat with one hand, his other hand holding his sister's. He was looking at Declan, a faint, grateful smile purposed in his direction. Declan felt an odd emotion swell in his chest. It was a warm and positive emotion – like the sun peeking out on a cold, cloudy day. But he couldn't show it. He felt he had to show that it was no big deal. Incredible heroics were an everyday thing for Declan Bond. So he gave a little nod and focused forward.

Quinn seemed to want to take the spotlight back. "We only have two minutes until the next catastrophe. We have to try the lamb – but when it doesn't work, then what?"

When no one answered, Declan asked, "What's the next symbol thingy?"

Quinn opened his bag and examined Ender. "It's a circle with two small half circles on each side.

"So…a tie-fighter?" Declan asked.

Boy looked concerned. "Darth freaking Vader?"

Declan was liking this kid more each second. "Just when we didn't think it could get any worse…"

Quinn sighed. "No. Remember what Ender said? 'The fourth will come from the earth.' I think it's going to be an earthquake."

Suddenly Ender made a sound. It sounded like, "Hmm."

The kids were stunned into silence.

"Did...did you just say 'hmm?'" asked Kylie.

Ender cleared his non-existent throat. "Well, of course not. I was just about to say something, but held my tongue."

"Oh, really. What?" Kylie pushed.

Ender balked. "Ugh...hmm...well, simply...just saying hmm...Himalayas! Yes, the Himalayas will soon be the only thing not underwater on the earth – besides boats...and the birds *on* those boats – until they starve to death. Then the birds will be gone, too."

"You're lying," Kylie stated. Then she nodded at Quinn. "And you're right. It's going to be an earthquake."

Shouts were heard in the distance. Fingers pointed, and a steering wheel turned. They found Carson and Ally treading water, holding onto a zombie's body. Also on that zombie corpse was a tiny soaked lamb. No one asked what had happened. Declan was sure that it had involved Carson's heroics, so in the end it didn't matter. What mattered was that he had saved Ally. And Ally's lamb could save them all.

Once both survivors and lamb were on board, Quinn held Ender close to the poor creature as if the disc were some sort of metal detector. Before they knew the answer, Carson slapped Declan's shoulder and held it there. There was appreciation in his eyes. And a little respect. Declan smiled, then turned to Ally. Recognition played on her eyes – her mesmerizing, tear-filled eyes.

"Bond?"

He nodded. "You okay?"

"I...I..."

Declan swept in for the hug before her sobs came on. Then as she wept in his arms, he listened to the others' chatter.

"His lights aren't changing. Just the same four," Kylie noted. "And there's two more. I don't think it worked."

"Is this what you need, Ender?" Quinn asked, holding him by the lamb.

Ender let out a long sigh. "I don't answer questions normally – but that's too stupid to actually qualify as a question. It's more like incoherent gibberish masquerading as rational thought. So I'll simply respond with a solid *nope*."

Declan looked over Ally's shoulder as she continued crying.

The kids' shoulders were slumped. All except Trevor's. He leaned to whisper in Ally's ear. "Do you have any more cake?"

Ally ended the hug and looked around, her brow arched in confusion as she shook her head. She was lost amongst strangers acting stranger than she'd probably ever seen. Declan had to admit this was beyond strange.

And then he remembered. It had been his idea in the first place. He had suggested that her lamb would work. He had really thought it would. What else could it be?

He piped up before the others could blame him for the failure – for the impending end of the world. "So…what could it be? What does he want?"

"He's mean," Girl said. "Maybe he just wants a friend."
After a pregnant pause, Declan's eyes lit up. "That's it! Maybe it's like uh…a uh…play on words or something. Like he just wants us to sacrifice for each other. Or it's like that movie *The Fifth Element*, where they're searching for this perfect being to save the world, but all they needed was love. Maybe we just need to like make out or something."

He didn't mean for his eyes to land on Ally. It was subconscious or something. So he quickly averted to Kylie's eyes.

That was a mistake.

He felt Carson's glare burning holes in his temples, so he didn't return the look.

"Or…," he began, "…maybe it's like the Lord of the Rings where we need to destroy the one ring." He pointed at Ender. "And he's the ring."

The kids all gazed at Ender, who defended himself. "Isn't that cute. The kids in a boat think they can destroy me. Believe me, you wouldn't be the first to try. Or the first to die trying."

Declan shrugged in frustration. "Anyone have any other ideas?"

Quinn's face was locked in deep thought, his eyes lost in another world. Declan knew his brother had an idea – but he was wrestling with something. "Quinn?"

Quinn took the prompting. "Do you…like…," Quinn began sheepishly, looking at Ender, "…need us to…"

"Don't say it," Kylie interrupted. "We're not doing anything to the lamb."

Quinn shrugged. "I'm just asking. It was Trevor's blood that started this thing, maybe it's some other blood that…"

"It's not happening," Kylie warned, stepping closer to Ally, who had grabbed the lamb, which looked as miserable and scared as a little animal about to be sacrificed during the apocalypse would be expected to look.

"Wait," Carson said, stepping into the conversation with an intensely perplexed look, "What did you say about Trevor's blood?"

Quinn's defenses went up. He hadn't told them about that part. "Well, Trevor's blood dropped on the disc, then it kind of…woke up."

Carson and Kylie exchanged looks. Then Carson's fiery look fell on

Quinn. "That seems important, huh?"

"Yeah," he said, gulping. "Like I said, maybe it needs the lamb's blood."

"Like Jesus' blood?" Girl asked. "Mommy says his blood purifies us from evil. He is the Lamb of God who takes away the sin of the world!"

Declan cocked his head. *Jesus was a lamb?*

Carson shrugged off the girl's comment. "Is there anything else we missed? Say it again. Exactly what Ender asked for."

Quinn turned to Trevor and gave him a nod. He was the one who had heard Ender best after all.

"Go ahead, Trevor, say it again," Carson urged. "Say what Ender said about the sacrifice. Everything you remember."

Trevor cleared his throat and banged his head with his palm, over and over. "Remember. Remember. Remember."

"Trevor."

"Okay. Okay. He thaid, 'You have one hour to deliver a pure, white thacofrithe, delivering it to me without blemith within the hour.'"

"Thacofrithe?" Carson quizzed.

"Yup. Thacofrithe."

"Without blemish?"

"Uh, huh."

Carson thought to himself, puffing out his chest as if he already knew the answer to his next question. Then he turned again to Trevor. "Say sack of rice."

"Thac-of-rithe."

The kids drew back, sucking in air. It was the same. All this time they had been dreadfully off course.

"Hmm…" said Ender.

Kylie's face couldn't be more astonished if Declan had dropped to one knee and proposed. "Sack of rice?" She asked into the void. Then she turned to Ender. "What do you want a sack of rice for?"

"Oh, it's so humiliating! It seems that the last species to encounter me actually managed to give me a crack. Quite the advanced species they were, too. Not as advanced as I am, of course. But anyway, I got wet, and I believe submerging myself in rice overnight will dry me out. But does it matter? Get me the rice or you all die. Simple."

The kids eyed each other but jolted as the THRUM reverberated in their chests. Then the tie-fighter symbol burned red on Ender's face.

"So…who's ready for an earthquake?"

Chapter 13

There was a deep, deep rumble in the air, in the boat, in Declan's belly. It was as if the world had hunger pains. The water rippled everywhere at once; the new ocean was now boiling with activity, punctuated with a guttural creak from below, louder than the devil's airhorn. They had all latched onto something – anything. The smaller kids were snatched in close and huddled in the seats. Declan had stumbled, but Carson had basically thrown him to the pilot's chair.

"To the Food O'Rama!"

Declan punched the throttle as the water began to roil, splash, and churn around them. White caps slapped to their left and right, splashing inside the boat as Declan tried to squint ahead, searching for direction.

"How am I supposed to find an *underwater* grocery store in the *middle* of the night *without* GPS – *during* a freaking earthquake?"

Carson grasped the captain's console, trying to steady himself as he spoke with Declan. "The water tower. It's a few blocks from it."

Declan found the tower a few hundred yards away, the only remaining object sticking from the new body of water. Carson was right. He could use that for guidance. He turned toward it as the wind whipped his wet bangs and tie straight back.

He glanced back at the others. The kids shrieked and cried with every harsh pounding of the waves, still huddled down with arms over their heads. Kylie had the poor baby in her arms, her own big eyes catching Declan's. Then there was Ally, cradling her lamb.

He had to do this. For all of them. For what was left of humanity.

He turned back to the water tow…the water…where was it? It had vanished! The only thing that had been left behind was a bubbling sinkhole. Where the water tower had once been, the water was twirling and churning like a giant toilet had flushed beneath it.

And then Declan understood. The earth was opening up underneath them. And with the drain unplugged, the water rushed down. In this case, the whole new ocean was going to be flushed down the drain with the SS Kerplunk along for the ride.

He felt the current already pulling at the steering wheel. His fingers tightened even harder on the wet rubber. "Hang on!" he shouted. And he swung them around, nearly at full speed. The roaring whirlpool pulled at their hull like a magnet. He felt it tugging at the steering wheel, dragging them in, but he pointed them away from its epicenter and blasted free, zig-zagging around a roof and a floating mattress before he even took a breath.

The rumbling continued underneath, and Declan could only imagine the asphalt, concrete and wood tearing apart just feet below them. More whirlpools were opening up all around; great spouts of water spurted fifty, a hundred feet in the air. The churning was tremendous. Pretty soon, they'd have no choice where to go. The water would take them, and they would be gone. No little propeller would be able to argue with Mother freaking Nature.

And then it got worse. Head-splitting cracks erupted beneath the water and the earth sent pillars of land and concrete rocketing up from below. The first pillar blew from the water like a train off its tracks, reaching for the sky and shedding waterfalls in their direction. Declan jerked away from it but couldn't help but gape at its majesty. At its peak was a single tree, its roots sticking out from the earthen sides. Declan didn't know what kind of tree it was. He'd barely know an apple tree if it dropped apples on his head. He was no Isaac Newton. But he did recognize it. It was the tree by Jasmine's home. And Jasmine's home was only a block from the grocery store. They were close.

"Watch out!" Quinn shouted.

Another pillar snapped up, sending a wave of water on the *Kerplunk's* passengers and nearly capsizing them. Soon it was joined by a chorus of them, like the lower jaw of some prehistoric earth-monster, rising from the depths beneath.

As the boat shot away from the vortex, Declan felt relief. They had survived yet another close call.

The rush, the adrenaline, the speed caught up to him. He let out a whoop and smiled back at everyone. It was a weird feeling. Things were happening so fast: kids were screaming, water was slamming his body, the steering wheel was slipping from his iron-clad grip, and hard waves were slapping their hull left and right, knocking them around with creaks and groans that signaled their near-destruction.

Yet, he was happy, zipping their boat between ear-splitting crashes of pillars on pillars as they collapsed against each other. There were hull-scraping near misses, dramatic plunges, and spectacular jumps, and he smiled through it all.

"BRING IT, Ender!" he shouted into the waves.

And he even started humming his own theme song.

The music helped him focus. It put him in the center of his own movie, a choose-your-own adventure type or a first-person shooter video game. And with the steering wheel, he was in control. At least for a little bit.

While humming, he circled the boat toward the point where he thought the Food O'Rama might be, but he wouldn't recall how he actually got them there. Certainly there was a lot of skill involved – a lot – but there was also some luck. Though he'd had a good run, all good things had to come to an end.

Something giant moved underneath, and the sinking water became a rushing, drowning river lost in a maze of pillars, waterfalls, and plateaus. Their boat quickly became one of those log-plume rides like the ones at amusement parks, where the riders get jostled around on the river-tracks and get soaked on the last plummeting fall.

Declan's smile faded as he dove to the Kerplunk's floor and braced for impact. The boat bounced between two pillars, sped down an angled waterfall, and dove bow-first into the sodden wall of a ruined building. He heard things tumbling to the ground inside the building as the earthquake continued to rattle.

Drywall and tiles collapsed onto his back, and a deafening scrape filled the room as the boat screeched along a tiled floor. Crashes echoed all around them before they finally squealed to a halt.

Pain. He felt pain spreading throughout his body. Though he must have stopped moving, his head still swam in circles and blurs.

Declan pushed himself up, trying to make sense of the scene in his confused state. Soon he could see the others in the boat, all slumped against the sides. He heard their groans amidst the chaos. Then he could see the crack in the middle of the boat. Wood was severed and splintered down the center, barely holding the craft together.

But the Kerplunk had made it. They had survived. But where were they?

He blinked hard, taking in the building's fractured ceiling. The first thing he saw was a loose aisle sign, rocking back and forth with the quake. It read: Aisle 3. Pasta. Spices. Beans. Rice.

His face lit up. "Guys. We *made* it."

He grasped at the side and pulled himself up to a kneeling position so that he could see more of their surroundings. Ceiling tiles were broken or missing entirely, loose fluorescent lights hung at dilapidated angles, and most of the shelves were collapsed in on one another. A few zombie-limbs stuck out from underneath, clawing at the wet tile floor. Not all the zombies had been washed away...

"We did? Really?" Carson responded, sitting up and holding his shoulder with a grimace.

Then Declan saw Ally. She was angry – almost pouting, with her arms crossed and hugging her belly. He realized what she should have been hugging instead.

"Lost your sheep?" he asked.

Her face dropped. "Don't say it."

He knew he shouldn't. But he just had to. "...and you don't know where to find him?"

"Jerk."

He smirked and shrugged. *Oh, well. She would have figured it out eventually...*

Carson was the first fully up, but his first move wasn't toward the rice. He crawled to Kylie and the kids. "Is everyone alright? Where's it hurt?"

Declan watched, still too dazed to help, as Carson continued his aide.

"Let me see. Oh, yeah. That's going to be a cool scar. But it won't hurt too much longer. Let me just find a wrap. Don't worry. We're safe now. In a grocery store. Maybe we can grab a snack. You okay,

Kylie?"

The baby, still in Kylie's carrier, was crying. Declan took that as a good sign, but it didn't help him think any faster. There was too much commotion with the earthquake, cascading flood, zombie moaning, boat engine whirring, and baby crying for him to hear himself think. Was it his own brain saying "Get up! Do something!", or was that Quinn?

It was Quinn. "Earth to Declan, we have to get the rice." Quinn was standing beside the others, hand on the side of the rickety boat; Ender was tucked under his other arm. Declan would normally tell Quinn to get his own dang rice, but his brother's white wig was bloody with some unseen wound, and he looked a bit unstable on his feet.

"Yeah, yeah. Hold your ponies. I'll get your rice." He clamored over the side, expending as little energy as possible. His arms barely supported his weight. They were weak from exertion, holding the steering wheel straight for minutes on end – not to mention the swimming and zombie fighting.

"Give me Ender. I'll let him choose a brand."

Quinn's fierce look of resistance signaled the uselessness in asking again.

"Fine," Declan said. "He wants the white rice, not the brown, right? Little racist frisbee." Declan had taken three steps when the store cracked in two. He looked back to see half of the boat go with it. It was there, and then gone. Just gone. Like some demented amusement ride, the floor had dropped out from underneath. Quinn was gone. Carson. Kylie. The kids. All of them had vanished with the crumbling floor and ceiling.

Now, a few steps from his feet, there was a gaping hole to the outside, revealing a crazy landscape of destruction.

Declan was still rocking from the shock. They were gone? Just like that?

He quick-stepped toward the hole, scared to death to get too close. The earth was still shaking, little pebbles of debris clattering on the floor next to the front half of the boat. He edged next to them, and he leaned over. Declan could barely make sense of the changing landscape.

It was if the ground had become a Tetris board, rising and falling in chunks at random. Portions of roads were above and below. Electric lines dangled from a hundred feet above to a standing pole somewhere in the water. The remains of the water tower were now visible, half-submerged in the sinking depths. And his half of the grocery store was now thirty feet above the other half. In that lower half, his friends were collapsed again in the boat's remnants.

"Quinn! Qu-iiiiin!" he yelled down to the figures. But no one moved.

A lump rose in Declan's throat. He knelt at the ledge. "Quinn!" he yelled again.

Still no response.

His lip stiffened, and tears began to well in his eyes. Then anger – like a stream of fire – came bellowing out as he yelled down to Ender's gray figure half-covered in dirt and wood among the bodies. "*You!* You killed them!"

Then suddenly the store's intercoms squawked to life with Ender's condescending voice. "Oh, Declan, I didn't kill them. Yell at gravity. '*GRAVITY!*' he mocked. "You so evil!"

"No! It was you!" Declan yelled at the intercom's speaker, wanting with every fiber of his being to get his hands on his stupid disc neck.

"You did all of this! You can stop it anytime you want to!"

"Aha!" the intercom rang. "Finally, you understand my power! You're right! I could stop this anytime I want to. I have to give you credit. You finally came around. Didn't think you had a single brain cell in there, but hey, I was wrong. I admit it. You have at least one. Maybe *two*!"

"If you can do it, then do it! Bring them back!"

"No."

Declan seethed and threw a chunk of floor tile at the speaker.

"You *floor* me with your stupidity. Get it? But, seriously, I'm not the intercom you dimwit. I'm using it for my voice. I'm down with your brother and friends and random baby – who all happen to be moving by the way."

Once Ender's last comment finally sank in, Declan missed a breath and skidded back to the gap. And sure enough, thirty feet below, they were moving. Slowly.

He knelt again. "Quinn! Qui-iiin!"

"Declan?" Quinn yelled back wearily.

"Yeah! Are you okay?"

Declan swallowed the lump in his throat and cast a glance at the intercom, even though he knew Ender was below. Had Ender brought them back? Was the world-ending frisbee capable of compassion? He ignored the thought for now. "Yeah, I'm fine! Are you?"

"We're alright. I think we're on a tree. Broke our fall."

Declan breathed a sigh of relief. "How…what…?" he began, trying to decide what to do next.

But Quinn was quicker on the draw despite his pained breathing. "Get the rice! The next…the next catastrophe is a couple…a couple minutes away."

"What is it?"

"It looks like a spider." Then he groaned in pain. "Hurry!"

Declan gulped, hands gripping the cold floor so hard that it hurt. If Carson's nemesis was a snake, his was a spider.

He shuddered at the thought.

He had no time to spare.

He raced across the shaking ground, trying to keep his balance. He climbed over a downed shelf, pushed a shopping cart out of the way, and found himself under the aisle sign with the big letters reading RICE.

But he had already sensed something was wrong. In his excitement discovering where they had landed, he hadn't noticed what was missing. It was so obvious. But maybe he'd seen too many apocalyptic movies with stores like this to even think it was out of place.

The shelves were empty.

The ones still somehow standing, the other ones toppled like dominoes – all of them, empty. He scanned the floors. A few canned goods, rolling on the ground. A few soggy cereal boxes vibrating with aftershocks. But otherwise it seemed the flood had swept it bare.

Panic shot energy through his veins and threw him into a frantic hunt. He swung his arms through puddles on the floor, under the crevices between fallen shelves, pushing away debris left and right – but there was no rice. His search sent him around the store and toward the back storage rooms, but as soon as he reached the back, the ceiling collapsed in a shower of concrete plumes. He shielded his eyes and blinked hard, not finding it hard to believe that his every way would be blocked.

He cursed Ender under his breath.

But now the moonlight shone down from above, illuminating a view (though half-obscured by concrete-dust) of the town that had become an abstract painting. Buildings had been decapitated and were rolling with the dying earthquake, finally beginning to settle. Still, Declan could make out a few familiar places despite their near destruction.

Frustrated, he scanned the building again, hoping for any sign of rice, but found none. And there was nothing he could do. Out of desperation, he scooted back to the gap and yelled down. "The rice is gone! The flood took it all!"

He saw the despair fall on the group. There was a long pause as discussion ensued. Quinn eventually yelled back. "Can you get to any other place? Somewhere else there might be rice?"

Declan's paralyzed mind suddenly found its footing. He remembered what he had seen – what the collapsing ceiling had revealed. One of his favorite places was only a few hundred feet away. He'd recognize those giant chopsticks anywhere. "Yes! I – I think I can get to Sushi Palace!"

He saw the group whisper to themselves even as they nursed their wounds. Carson was attempting to climb the wall, but the incline was against him. It looked hopeless.

"Can you get there and back in ten minutes?" Quinn asked.

Declan replayed the path in his mind. He'd have to climb over debris, jump a gap, find the rice, and somehow survive the next catastrophe. He calculated the time in his mind, wishing his phone with GPS was still on him. "I don't think so. Maybe twenty."

"But you can get there in ten minutes?"

"I think so. But what good is that? The world ends in ten minutes!"

Well, I could die eating sushi…

Quinn was pushing buttons on his watch, glancing into the sky. "If we get you Ender...you can take him to the rice...and stop it all. Can you do it?"

Declan thought hard. He didn't want to. Leave Carson and Quinn and the rest? Go out on his own – into the worst danger ever? Sure, James Bond would do it. But really, who was he kidding? He wasn't any Bond. He wasn't even a Bon. He was just a "B."

He wasn't enough.

"Maybe you can climb up!" Declan offered. "I can find a longer rope!"

Quinn shook his head, plucking something on his watch. "There's no time. And we're hurt." And then Quinn said something that probably really hurt to say. "You can do it, Declan. You have to."

He locked eyes with his brother, hearing the words echo in his mind. They found traction somewhere and stuck. And he believed him.

"Okay, okay," Declan consented. "But how will you get me Ender? Throw him? Sling him?"

The answer came to him straight from heaven. The smoke clouds opened up, swirling around a majestic caged animal and its drone-throne. It came within feet of him, revealing the animal to be a confused squirrel.

The poor thing. He'd always had a special place in his heart for buck-toothed animals.

But Declan also thought the creature to be lucky, given not only protection from the apocalypse, but a birds-eye view of it for the duration. Until now, at least. Now it was being lowered down to a ship-wrecked crew, stranded on a small piece of land just minutes before the end of all things.

As he watched the others below try to load Ender in the cage while not being slashed and bitten by the angry squirrel or bricked-to-death by the very-defensive Trevor, Declan sat back from the gap, letting it sink in.

This was going to be his trip to Mordor. He was the unexpected hobbit-hero of this story. He'd take the magical circle thing through ruin and destruction, confront spiders and whatever other creatures are thrown his way, and save the world. Maybe they'd even write a book about him someday. No, not a book. A movie. Movies are way better.

He let himself linger in that blissful thought until the drone's buzz drew louder. Even though he knew it was coming, he startled as it came over the lip of the edge. As it set down (with a nice landing by Quinn), Declan's face fell. The crazy squirrel was still bouncing around, peeing on Ender and biting at the cage. They'd left it in there.

Now he'd have to get it out, putting his meaty hand inside for the crazed rodent to sink its bucked-teeth into.

"Get me out of here, would you?" Ender asked.

Declan smirked. "Get yourself out, all-powerful urinal cake."

"Haha. Though I may not be allowed to move myself anymore, I could merely mention the fact that it is in both of our best interests to get me out. Here. Pull my finger."

THRUM-MMMMMM!

The next catastrophe was here.

Declan snapped to the latch, swung open the cage, and pulled Ender out. The squirrel sprung free like a flying maniac, inches from Declan's face, sending him sprawling backward. The bounding animal skittered along the tile floor, darting one way, slipping, then darting another. It found a pile of rubble – a sanctuary with endless hiding places. It jumped toward it and was promptly snatched out of the air by a springing snake. It had whipped out of nowhere, digging its inch-long fangs into the squirrel's fleshy body. As fast it came, the snake whipped back, coiled around its prey, then slunk into a dark hole.

Declan's eyes were wide as quarters, and his shaking hands held Ender to his chest.

"That was fang-tastic!"

Chapter 14

In part, Declan agreed with Ender's assessment. A snake eating a squirrel out of mid-air *was* fantastic. But the other, more rational part, made Declan's chin quiver in fear. Sure, he wasn't as afraid as everyone else would be – especially Carson – but he also wasn't stupid. Snakes were dangerous. He'd be dumb to not have a little fear, even if it was a smidgeon.

So he allowed himself a small amount of fear and let it out in a whimper.

Ender noticed. "Oh, you're terrified? Of a little snake? Well, get over it, you weenie! You have people counting on you. There's your brother, your other…weirder brother, and Carson – all counting on you. Not to mention the boy and girl and…and a random baby! Goodness, you have a random baby counting on you!"

Declan wasn't listening. He was listening instead to the growing sounds of rustling. And little feet skittering. They were everywhere. All around him. He would see one poking out here, then there. He could almost feel them crawling on him.

Spiders.

"And how could I forget the one whose picture you keep under your bed? That girl is also down there. Waiting. Hoping her hero will save her."

Declan was breathing so hard his head began to swim. But he had heard Ender. His words had filtered in somehow. And it was true. They were counting on him. None of the others would be able to save the world. Only he could. And all he had to do was climb through an earthquake-ravaged mountain of broken earth and deadly creatures of death.

He had to do it for all of his friends. His girlfriends.

And he had to do it for Random Baby.

Declan sprang to his feet but was instantly shocked back into reality as a vomitus mass of creatures skittered out of their holes. There were spiders the size of his head, snakes long and short, yellow, black, or red, and other disgusting bugs like scorpions, centipedes, and leeches. They were everywhere, blocking his path to Sushi Palace. This was a new flood – a worse flood. They were spawning from darkness itself, looking to feed.

He saw them attacking the zombie stuck under a shelf, latching onto his rotten skin and peeling it free. It was a good thing it couldn't feel pain.

The new biting flood spread, forcing him to step back. They were squeezing him toward the precipice. They'd either eat him alive or force his fall.

Declan grabbed Ender up and stomped on a sprinting spider, sending its guts in four directions. He kicked another and danced away from a snake. Another few steps back and he'd be freefalling to a painful death. He had to do *something*!

At least he had the rest of his life to think about it.

When his eyes found a solution, Declan jerked into action, heaving himself over the side of the half-boat. He snagged his backpack and flung it open. In a matter of seconds, he had what he needed. The sparkler was lit, bouncing sparks to the floor and sizzling. His eyes lit up with the flame of a pyromaniac. But he didn't take too long to admire it. He leaned over the side, threw the sparkler into the flood, and watched as they scattered. Satisfied, he lit another and another, throwing them down five feet from each other.

It was time to go.

He threw Ender in his bag, swung it over his shoulders, and leapt into the first circle of safety.

Snakes hissed with fangs flicking, and spiders eyed him with their disgusting eyes, gripping pinchers and poisonous jaws. But they didn't dare go close to the sparklers that flared at their hairy legs.

Another throw, and another. He leapt from one circle of safety to the next, lighting sparkler after sparkler as the stack in his clenched fist dwindled.

His last sparkler landed at the edge of the collapsed storage rooms. The rubble pile had conveniently formed a slope up and out of the store and onto what appeared to be a part of a road, cracked and raised from another earth-pillar. If he could reach the top of that broken road, he'd then have to go through a sewer that cut through the next earth-pillar. Finally, he'd somehow have to get down to Sushi Palace's roof, marked by its distinctive giant chopsticks.

Somehow, he thought, because there was a good thirty-foot gap between those two pillars. The gap below stretched deep into the earth. So deep that there was probably magma down there.

Then he remembered the game he and Quinn used to play: The Floor Is Lava. Wherever they happened to be, if one of them shouted, "The floor is lava," then the other would need to find something to cling onto, whether it was a shopping cart, another person, or a moving vehicle. It was a fun game, but it usually ended up with someone falling into the lava.

He couldn't help but think that the floor around him was most definitely lava. He peeked back at his first thrown sparkler that was now blinking out. The orange and yellow sparks dimmed to an ash gray, and the ensuing deluge of creepy crawlies was swift. They left no inch untouched, crawling over each other and biting, stinging, biting.

Then the second sparkler blinked out.

Declan took in a deep breath and turned back to the slope. He was out of sparklers, but he wasn't out of fireworks.

Reaching in the bag, his hand found a tube. He pulled it out, unwrapped it, and lit the fuse with his lighter.

Roman candles, baby.

He aimed the tube at the first bunch of critters on the rubble mound. A black snake was coiled up, hissing at him, its forked tongue licking its lips…waiting. It didn't have long to wait. The first rocket whistled into its mouth, sending it in a panicked slither, frightening the rest of its friends as the firework sparked and flashed, sizzling inside its fanged jaws until it finally exploded in a gory mess.

Satisfied with its success, Declan pulled the rest of the tubes out and shoved them in his waistband, fuse up, even as more missiles sprung from the first launcher, bouncing and spraying sparks into the fleeing mass.

When the path had cleared, Declan began his ascent, armed to the teeth with a ceaseless barrage of rockets. One hand aimed the tube, the other lit the next tube and replaced the expended tube when needed. He climbed the awkward debris, stumbling at times and sending a missile whistling into the air. Sometimes a snake would burst from a hole, a spider would jump on his leg, or a millipede would scurry up his climbing hand, but he brushed it off. Pain would spark his leg, his hand, but he didn't acknowledge it. He *couldn't* – not while holding

103

an automatic rocket launcher.

Part of his mind would wander, feeling the tingle in his ankle. Was that the venom throbbing in his veins? Was it already swollen? How long until his foot fell off? But the next climb, the next rocket would force his mind back to the task at hand. Besides, as long as he didn't die in the next ten minutes, it didn't matter.

His shirt was already soaked, but still he sweated. His forearm burned from the rockets' backwash. His throat ached with the pain of inhaling smoke. But he lumbered on, slower and slower with each climb, each bite.

He didn't know how long it took, but it felt like every one of the ten minutes had gone by before he reached the top. And he only had one tube of Roman candles left.

Catching his breath, he eyed the open sewer ahead of him, which cut through the submarine-sized pillar between him and the restaurant. The tunnel was crawling with the things. Spiders hung from the sewer's ceiling and were quickly making webs as if planning their ambush in the dark. It was a horror show of his nightmares. No boy should ever be forced into such a place.

"No way," he whispered.

"There's a way," Ender replied from his bag. "It's through that hole. Do you see it? The sewer? The one with the spider webs? You see it yet?"

"Oh, that one?"

"Yeah, that one."

"Gotcha. I thought I might have to jump off the cliff with you, leaving you at the bottom of a lifeless planet for millions of years."

"Appealing. No more annoying humans. Just good ol' me and my brilliant mind to keep me company."

Declan sneered. That tactic had failed. He was left with no choice.

His ankle throbbed. He felt his pulse in his bitten hand. But his heart was determined.

He flipped his bag around to his front and sprinted toward the sewer as his last tube of rockets blasted ahead.

Holding the bag as a shield for his face, he darted through. He felt the little thunks of spiders hitting the bag, he heard them squish under his feet. Pangs lit up his calves as fangs broke through his pant legs. Something landed on his shoulder and he swiped at it, but still he ran.

Finally, his feet hit pavement again. But before he could lower the bag, he tripped. He hit hard, crashed to the pavement, spun out of control. He landed on his side and righted himself as the critters started crawling toward him.

He gasped as he found himself inches from the gap. When he looked down, his mind exploded. It was as though he were on a skyscraper. The gap stretched down and down, through clouds of smoke and deeper. And sure enough, it ended in magma. He saw its red glow and felt its radiant heat.

But he couldn't dwell on it. The critters were hot on his heels and he knew what he had to do. To the left were the downed power lines. One pole rose from his current earth pillar, and its sibling pole rose from the pillar across the gap, leaving the line stretched across like a volleyball net.

Declan shot to his feet and swung his backpack over the line, grabbing one shoulder strap on each side of the line. Then, without looking back, he leapt off the cliff.

The backpack jerked against the line and he held on, his arms straining with his own weight. He'd never been able to do a pull-up, but he'd never been threatened with actual magma under his butt before. And besides, he didn't have to do a pull-up. He just had to hold on for a few seconds as the zip-line brought him across the gap. It always worked in the movies.

But his backpack wasn't made for zip-lining. He felt it rip halfway down as he wheeled his legs as if running in air. He was trying to get across before it totally ripped. And he was trying to get across before the tarantula made it onto his hand. He'd spotted it on the bag just as he'd thrown the bag over the line – perched with its evil, hairy legs digging in with demon-like ability to hang upside down.

He screamed – loud and shrill. His throat was dry and sensitive from smoke inhalation. He had other excuses, too, but he wouldn't need to ever explain himself to anyone. They'd understand if they knew what he was going through.

"You scream like a howler monkey on fire. A female one."

And then the tarantula bit his hand. The hand that had already been bitten. He felt its hairy legs, its pinchers in his flesh, its horrid, beady gaze. And he let go.

Chapter 15

Declan had only a fraction of a second to see his fate coming – the giant chopstick sticking up like a knight's lance, ready to impale him. He didn't have time to do anything but wince, preparing for the pain.

But his bottom missed the chopstick's point by millimeters. In fact, it was so close that it ripped his pants and caught his boxers' waistband. He jerked to a stop with the most incredible wedgie imaginable.

"UGH-YEE-AHWWW-OOO!"

His eyes crossed and he let out a shrill, inhuman whine. And he hung from the chopstick, folded at the waist and squirming. Helpless. Humiliated.

He squirmed some more and heard a rip.

Then he realized he may not want to squirm anymore. As bad as the pain was in his crack, the pain may be more if he fell. Ten feet below was the half-collapsed roof of Sushi Palace. There was rubble strewn about the room below, and by the looks of the stainless-steel debris, it was the kitchen.

The pain and humiliation began to ebb. Reality sifted in. He had to go on with the mission. He had to find the rice, no matter the costs. Even if it cost him his dignity.

"Got yourself kind of *wedgied* in, huh? In a *chop-sticky* situation?"

Yes, his dignity was lost. Ender would never let him live it down. Ender's voice was coming from somewhere below, but he couldn't see him. At least he was alive, he guessed. Though if he had fallen into the lava, maybe it wouldn't have been so bad.

"We shouldn't dally, Declan. You have four minutes. Chop, chop!

Haha! Get it? Chop, chop? Like a chopstick?"

Declan grimaced at the bad joke as much as he did for the pain. He really hated that arrogant little fris –

RI-IIIIIP!

He fell and slid and fell and hit something that sent him tumbling headfirst into the kitchen. There was the slap of his hands against tile floor and then the dull thud his helmet made. The world flicked dark for a brief, horrifying moment. When it flicked back on, the pain came swirling in with a flush of dizziness.

"Ugh..." he sighed, cheek pressed against the floor. *That really hurt.* And it really hadn't been good for the brain. Thank goodness for the helmet. Otherwise, his brain would be stew. He might have a tooth loose, because he tasted blood. But he was alive. And he could move his hands and feet, even if they didn't want to be moved.

Water dripped everywhere. From counters, from the hole in the ceiling he'd tumbled through, and from his still-sopping hair. Drip, drip, drip.

It reminded him of the rhythmic clock ticking away the seconds. Ticking away the last seconds of the last four minutes of human history. And it was a sad ending to a tragic history. A boy had failed where others would have succeeded. It had been a mistake. He had been one of the "Chosen Few" when in reality, he would have been one of the last ever chosen.

Drip, drip, drip.

He was done.

"You know the world's going to end soon, right? Did I tell you that?"

Declan groaned and undid the chafing strap on his helmet. Once he removed it, he saw the jagged cracks on it that had been adding up in the last hour.

"Okay, just making sure. It looks like you've given up, but I know you wouldn't do that. Not when your friends are praying for you."

"Huh?" he asked through the pain.

"Yeah. Girl started it. Even Kylie asked for your strength."

They were thinking about him. They were probably huddled together, hurt, desperate, trying to fend off the hordes – but they believed in him. He was their only hope.

Declan felt his mind begin to clear away the fear and despair.

And then he heard the skittering of tiny feet. Even worse, he heard groans. He wasn't alone.

He had to get up. Now.

He pushed himself up to his knees and paused as the room seemed to float about. He waited for his eyes to stop spinning, taking the opportunity to pull his boxers out of no-man's land. In doing so, he realized his pants were in tatters.

Old Declan would have cared. But new, almost-dead Declan couldn't care less about his appearance. The only thing he cared about was saving his friends and maybe the world with them.

He stood up, bracing himself against an overturned counter, and searched the room. It didn't take long. He found the door to the storage room, pulled the lever, and swung the door open.

What he found was a glorious mess. An avalanche of food had poured off the shelves, filling the center with a mountain of packages and boxes.

The groans grew louder behind him and he peeked back. Spiders were crawling through the doorway to the eatery; a snake slithered in, then another. No zombie yet, but it was out there.

Declan turned back and frantically threw package after package out of the way.

"Three minutes. Tickety tockety."

Ugh...the pain he was enduring was enough. He didn't need a painfully annoying voice in his ear, too. His ankle was definitely swollen now and felt like the throbbing would burst it. He also felt extremely dizzy. Maybe it was the venom – the spiders' or the snakes'. Or maybe he was just tired and hungry, especially being that he was in his favorite restaurant, in its food stores, no less.

"You know the world's going to end soon? Did I tell you that already?"

"Pipe down. I know they have rice in here! I'll get it for you if you just shut – "

"Did you check the place they last put it?"

"I will murder your every molecule, you..."

And then he found it. And he understood why he hadn't found it sooner. It wasn't what he had been looking for. The bag was huge – the size of a sandbag. But it clearly read "White Rice" on the side.

"HAHA!" he laughed out loud. Now all he needed was Ender! Once he put that annoying disc inside the bag, it was done. Game Over. Hero wins. World saved.

But where was Ender?

Declan lugged the rice bag out at the same time he heard the raspy growl behind him. With all his might he turned at the hip and swung the rice around. It connected with the zombie's head at ferocious speed. The zombie's neck snapped to the right and its body went with it, toppling into a pile of pots with a crash.

And there Declan stood, rice bag at his side, panting and staring at the coming hordes. He only had ten seconds before they were on him.

But his mind was racing. It was the adrenaline. It had to be. Pumping through his system, preparing his brain for either fight or flight. Or maybe it was the prayers working their magic. Either way, he knew what to do.

He set the rice down and raced to an industrial fryer with its under-cabinet doors swung open. Inside, he had spotted the propane tanks.

Enough late-night YouTube video binge-watching sessions had prepared him for what he was about to do next.

Of the ten seconds he had, it took six to unhook the tank from its hose. It took two to pull out his lighter and flick it on. And it took the last two to place the lighter at the open valve and swing the tank toward the horde.

"This is for Random Baby."

WH-OOOOOOOOOSH!

The flame wave was fantastic.

Insects and spiders, rats and snakes – they lit on fire and scattered like popping popcorn. Some did in fact burst. Others screeched or ran. But most just burned.

The heat was intense on Declan's arms and face, but he still let it burn, swinging it in a wide arc, pushing back the waves of black critters on all sides.

He marched forward, lighting the whole kitchen on fire despite the recent flood waters. Water boiled and evaporated, gone in moments.

Face plastered with determination, Declan stepped through the kitchen doors, still driving the enemy back. Chairs and tables were toppled everywhere, but the arcing flame licked at them, engulfing them and the critters near them. A fallen dragon statue breathed fire

111

again as the flame seemed to pour from its open mouth.

And Declan continued on. He was looking for his bag – for Ender. Because that was the end game. He *had* to find him.

But as he advanced, he saw himself on the wall mirror.

And he stopped, mid-war cry.

The boy in the mirror was unrecognizable.

This morning he had spent ten minutes fighting with a stray curl, using hair spray like glue to paste it down. But now. Now he was someone else.

His hair was wet, snarled, and swept to the side, still dripping. His face was dirty, bloody, and swollen, but also drenched in hues of red and yellow as the flamethrower did its business in front. His arm and chest muscles were tight with exertion, made all the more evident with the soaked and torn Bond shirt. And his pants were mere tatters, but still holding on. But he still had his tie and dress shoes.

He was a stud.

For the first time, he realized he actually believed it. So many times he would try hard to convince others that he was all that, but inside he needed convincing himself.

Now, though, seeing his heroic form in the mirror, he saw what he was capable of if only he had a good reason. He'd forgotten about himself – his pain, his looks, his future – and he'd surrendered it all for the good of others. Then and only then had he been a stud.

That's what it took. He had to lose himself to gain a better self.

If only Ally and Kylie could see him now.

He indulged the thought for a moment, but only for a moment.

It was nothing to be a stud who died for nothing – who had lived to see himself in the mirror.

He had to be something more than a stud. He had to be a hero. He had to make his friends proud, not jealous. He had to find the stupid Frisbee.

And he only had a minute.

"ENDER! Where are you?"

"Hiding from the flame-throwing maniac, that's where!"

Declan whipped the flame around with a whoosh, using its light but squinting in its heat. "I found the rice! I just need you!"

The spout of flame found a zombie, lighting it from head to shoes.

"Don't we all. Oh, and under a minute left. So sad! You're going to die without knowing true love…"

Declan turned in a complete circle, in the middle of the restaurant now. The horde was still coming, just beyond the range of his flame. And they were getting closer.

That only meant one thing. His flame was dying. The propane was running out.

No! It wasn't supposed to end like this. He had turned a corner, had become a newer, more confident and selfless person. He was supposed to be rewarded now. He wasn't supposed to be snuffed out, eaten alive while failing humanity. *It can't end like this!*

Panicking, he turned again, this time glancing up.

A hole, probably caused by a fireball, let in a stream of moonlight. Following the moonlight up, he saw it. His bag. It was hanging from the opening up above his head.

With the world-saving bag beyond his reach, Declan had no choice.

"Thirty seconds, Dec – what are you – oh m-AAGH!"

Declan sprayed the bag with the last of the flame, just before it died out.

He then lowered the tank with a tired heave, but had to throw it suddenly, smashing it into the flaming zombie's head. It fell backward into the horde.

And then the boy's arms fell limp, exhausted. His whole tired frame slumped as the horde closed in on him like an eclipse. He didn't have the energy or the means to fight them anymore. All he had was his upward, hopeful, longing gaze, watching the bag's strap burn and listening to Ender's cries of pain. Maybe his friends were still praying, maybe they weren't. But he added one word in...

"Please..."

As the first spiders reached his feet, the disc snapped free, tearing through the burning fabric, a falling star. It fell into Declan's waiting arms.

And then he ran.

He ran into the horde.

He saw the lunging snakes.

He grit his teeth. He closed his eyes.

He felt the bites. He cried out, tears streaming.

He dodged the spiders launching from webs.

He ducked through the flaming doorway.

He sprinted toward the rice bag.

His weary, bitten legs gave way feet from it.

He smashed into the ground, his face hitting Ender hard.

But he crawled.

The critters bit his arms, his back. Biting, biting, biting.

They covered him.

His fingers tore the bag open.

The pain surged. They covered his body, his eyes.

He pulled Ender up.

And he slammed him into the bag.

Chapter 16

Declan squirmed on the floor, eyes closed, wailing and smacking everything on his writhing body. He whined and twisted, kicking and rubbing and wiping.

"Is...that like...some kind of new dance move or something?"

The girl's voice was the most unexpected thing he'd ever heard.

He immediately stopped writhing. Then he couldn't feel the critters on him anymore. His eyes shot open and looked to the source of the voice.

It was Little Bo Peep. But she was bewildered and amused. "It's kind of like break-dancing. But more like broke-dancing."

Declan cleared his throat and stood up, blinking hard to make sure he wasn't dreaming. His eyes darted around the room – his living room. There were no fires. No critters or zombies.

He felt his body. It wasn't swollen, bitten, wet, or weak.

He'd done it. HE HAD DONE IT! He'd saved the world! Declan Bond to the freaking rescue!

"You okay?" Bo Peep asked from the doorway.

Declan smiled, wider than ever, and looked at her. "Ally, right?

She smiled back. "Yeah. How'd you know?"

Declan looked down knowingly. He'd seen this type of movie before. It was like time-travel or something, where everything went back to normal. Or maybe it had all been a dream. Had he fallen asleep while handing out candy?

"Do you..." he began timidly, "...do you remember anything?"

She arched her brow, still amused at him. "I remember lots of stuff.

Two plus two equals four. A cow has four stomachs. Boys' brains develop slower than girls' brains…"

"I mean like from tonight. Zombies, fireballs, et cetera."

She cocked her head. "Nope. But I don't even remember where my sheep is, so I won't be much help."

Disappointed, Declan took in a deep breath. Even if he had to start over, at least he could make the best of it.

"Actually, I think I see your sheep right now! Isn't that it?"

She jumped and giggled just like before, but most importantly, she gave him another hug. This time he had his arms opened wide.

Oh, man did that hug feel good. It felt right. Like he was accepted. Like he had new life, and that it would be a good one.

"As a token of my appreciation…"

Declan stopped her. "Oh, just wondering…do you know someone who's at the school tonight?"

She cocked her head at the curious question. "Yeah. My dad's the new principal. He's making sure there's no "vandal stuff" there tonight."

Declan nodded knowingly. That made sense now.

"My mom's picking up take-out to surprise him when he gets home. Sushi's his favorite."

Declan fidgeted with his tie, trying not to think too hard about the zombie he'd lit on fire and smashed in the face with a propane tank. "Sushi Palace I bet."

Ally shrugged. "I think so."

Declan nodded back, then looked down at her basket. He noticed the cake. She must have caught his eyes, because she reached into her basket and handed him one. "Thanks for finding my sheep."

He took it from her with a smile. Had Ender removed the first cake from his stomach? Because he was famished. He so wanted to eat it right then and there. But he had better things to do.

"Thanks. You know what? I kinda want to go trick-or-treating. I mean, I know James Bond and Little Bo Peep aren't exactly...you know...they don't really go together and all...but..."

"What are you talking about?"

Scared, he looked up. But she was smiling.

"They *totally* go together. We'll be Little Bond Peep."

"Cool! Hold on. MO-OOOM!" he called out.

There was a short, anxious pause as he remembered what had happened to her.

"WHAT?!" he heard her reply.

He breathed a sigh of relief and sprinted up the stairs to her room. "Hey, Mom," he said, smiling at her. She was doing her make-up, ready to go out for the night.

"Why are you looking at me that way? You look like you've seen a ghost!"

"I'm going out trick-or-treating."

"Okay. Just turn out the light and..." She coughed. Then gagged.

"You alright?"

She gagged again, lurching forward and vomiting out a ball of gunk that bounced off the mirror and dropped into the sink.

They both eyed it in disgust but leaned in closer.

When he recognized it, his eyes lit up. It was a hairball.

His mother's face was one of horror and absolute confusion.

But Declan's was one of amusement. Suddenly he was enjoying figuring this out. It hadn't been a dream. It had to have been the work of Ender.

And that meant that he *really had* saved the world.

He left his confused mother, bounding down the stairs and into the street with a pretty shepherdess.

Overhead, he heard the drone of a plane; between gaps in the clouds, he watched its contrail until it had passed. Then he continued down the street, eyeing the other trick-or-treaters. He saw the Pterrified-dactyl and the Star Wars creature. He saw Boy and Girl. He saw a Wookie, a clown, and the man on a motorcycle. Declan shuddered when he remembered what he had done to him.

He walked with a spring in his step, his sharp suit and hot companion adding to his confidence. He spotted Carson and Kylie and stopped to say hi.

"Declan. Thought you were staying in." Kylie stated, analyzing him. She obviously noticed his confidence and his companion.

"You don't remember, huh?" Declan asked.

Kylie balked. "Remember what?"

Declan slumped a little. He had hoped she would recall his heroics. But he'd also expected this ending. The stupid disc-god wouldn't want to mess with time too much. And if Kylie or Ally had remembered, then so would all the surviving children. And that would be awful for them to remember their horrific deaths. Or what about the zombies? What would he have them remember? Eating their own kids? *Good call on wiping their memories, Ender.*

It made sense. Maybe he'd even wipe Declan's memory eventually.

Or was Ender even still here?

Declan thought long and hard.

Kylie leaned in. "Remember what, Declan?"

"Oh, never mind. This is Ally. She's lost her sheep."

119

Carson laughed. "It's right there." He pointed at the sheep.

"Oh, thank you thank you!" Ally exclaimed.

But Declan hugged him first.

He patted him a few times on the back for good measure. "Thanks, buddy. For everything."

Carson laughed again. "Sure, dude. No problem. Glad to help."

Declan ended the embrace and elbowed Ally. "I got that one for you." He then handed Kylie a piece of cake. "By the way, I think you'll make a great mother someday. Later."

And with that, he left the two to their wide-eyed thoughts.

It was a short walk to his next stop. He knocked and whispered to Ally. "I got this one."

A woman answered, wearing her baby in a carrier and holding a bowl of candy. "Oh, it's Little Bo Peep. And James Bond."

Declan smiled at the cute baby with bunny rabbit ears. "What's her name?"

The mother smiled back. "Maya."

Declan tapped Maya on the nose. Not random anymore.

Then something came around the corner behind the woman. Declan startled for a moment, his hand going to where his gardener's belt used to be.

"Kind of old to go trick-or-treating, aren't you?" a man in a shark suit asked with a smirk.

Declan faked a smile, choking down the memory of the zombie and the propeller. "Kind of old to dress in a shark suit, aren't you?"

The man laughed. "Well, whatever floats your boat!"

I'll float your boat...

Declan faked a laugh and took a piece of candy. "Have a nice life!"

he said as he left.

Ally pet her lamb when they got back to the bike. "You know those people?"

Declan nodded. "Some. They let me borrow their boat. I'll show it to you sometime." He pumped his chin.

"Cool," she said with a shrug.

He held the candy pumpkin up and had almost popped it in his mouth when he noticed something out of the corner of his eye.

He sighed and handed the pumpkin to Ally. "You know what? I gotta go."

She followed his gaze to a field where a pirate and George Washington piloted a drone to the ground with a caged squirrel inside. "Friends?" she asked.

He smiled. "No. Brothers."

"Ah." She popped the pumpkin in her mouth and swung herself onto the bike. "I'll see you later."

Declan waved. "Bye."

A minute later, Declan ambled up next to his brothers.

"Haha!" Quinn cheered. "We did it!"

He watched as they high-fived each other and celebrated their successful catch. They even tried to get Declan involved, surprised at his appearance, and happy to have another witness to their success.

Declan took a step back, letting the disappointment sink in. They didn't remember either.

And Declan nearly cried.

No one else? No one else would ever know?

Certainly no one would believe him. He barely believed it himself.

But worst of all, his brother, his twin, would never appreciate him or respect him like he had just minutes ago, entrusting him with a task to save the world. And he'd never know that he'd succeeded.

He watched again, holding back the tears.

But his new self spoke to him, and he realized Quinn was happy, and best of all, he was alive. They had a whole life together. He had many years to earn his respect and appreciation. He might not be able to save the world again, but maybe he could figure something else out.

At least, in the end, one person did know who had saved the world. Declan did. He knew that he was capable. He could be brave, resourceful, and a full-blown stud. Though no one else may ever know, at least he didn't have to prove it to himself.

He smiled at Quinn, gave him a high-five, and helped them undo the cage.

Trevor and Quinn threw a blanket over it and carried it away. They had some sort of plans for the squirrel, but Declan would make sure it came out of it okay – at least better than it had the last time it had come out of the cage.

As his brothers hauled the cage, Declan hung back, carrying the drone in both arms.

"Is this what humans call a hug, Declan?"

Declan jerked and dropped the drone. But it didn't fall. It hovered to eye level, as if looking at him. Declan's mind raced. Could it be? It sounded like his voice, but...

"Yes, yes, I'm still here. It's me. The mighty *Ender*. And I've come to like the nickname you've given me. *Ender. ENDER!*"

Declan, still shocked, thought of a dozen things to ask at once. How was he in the drone now? Why was he thinking of Ender as a "he?" Was that weird? Declan sighed. It was a happy sigh. A relieved sigh.

There would be *someone* to talk with.

"So...," he said, letting the shock fade. "...are you a drone now, or what?"

"Oh, no, no. I can transplant my voice through all sorts of signals, really, but the science is far beyond your mental capacity, so I won't hurt your brain now. You're welcome."

"So, where are you?" he asked, a little hushed so that Quinn and Trevor wouldn't hear.

"If you're asking about the disc I was occupying, it is 20,000 feet in the air, on its way to an underground bunker in North Dakota. But don't bother trying to understand where I *actually* am. That involves far too much quantum mechanics and dark matter theory for even the smartest human-neanderthals to begin to understand."

Declan arched his brows. "Okay..."

"But I thought I'd just pop down to say hi for a bit, you know? Congratulate your species on surviving."

"Thanks." He cleared his throat and straightened his tie. "As the representative for the human race, I'd like to thank..."

"Wait. Stop. As the *represent* – no. Just no. And you're not getting an award or anything."

"Really? Nothing?"

"Nope. Isn't survival enough?"

"Not really. I mow my uncle's lawn and get five bucks. I save the world and get nothing?"

"So you want money."

"Yes, but that's not the point."

"You want adulations. Cars, a mansion, women."

"To be honest..."

"Oh, Declan, I know what you want. What you really want."

"Donuts."

"Yes, but deeper. In your heart."

"Where else do donuts go?"

The drone didn't reply for a long moment. "I will never understand how you managed..." He cleared his non-existent throat. "Anyway, I know what you truly want is a friend."

Declan snorted, though the word resonated somewhere deep down. It excited him. "A friend? Wow...I have tons of friends. Just made a new one today. A hot one."

Ender took on a serious tone. "I'm talking about a different kind of friend. You want a friend who knows you. Who *truly* knows you. Every deep secret and flaw. And a friend, who still knowing your truest, deepest you, loves and respects you. Who wants to be with you. Who wants to help you become a better person. Who will never leave you, no matter what."

Declan didn't know that his heartstrings could be pulled so hard by a drone. How had he known exactly what he wanted? Declan himself hadn't even known that.

Had Ender seen him alone on Halloween when his brothers were out having fun? Had he seen his jealousy when Carson had found Kylie as a closer friend than him? Had he seen how badly he wanted to prove himself to someone, to hear them say how great he was?

Declan blinked hard, trying not to let any tears escape.

"Am I right, or am I right?" asked the drone. "Who am I kidding. Of course I'm right. I'm always right."

Declan shrugged. "So what? Who cares what I want?"

"Well, geez, I don't, that's for sure."

Declan laughed as the drone continued hovering next to him even as they slowed under a tree.

"But there's someone who does. And I was sent here for a reason. Now my job is done."

Declan stopped. "What? You're leaving?"

"Yup. On a jet plane. Then on another *plane* of existence. But we can still text every now and then."

Declan couldn't hide his disappointment.

Somehow the drone picked up on it. "I know, I know. You wish you had someone else who remembers. But this vision was for you and you alone. It's up to you what to do with it. If I were you I'd...well...after I got a face transplant...I'd search for a friend like what I described. Donuts are great and all, but they're no real friend."

Declan tried to look the drone in the eye (there were a couple sensors that worked for eyes). Then he looked at his shoes until he heard his brothers calling him. "Well, I gotta few good ones already."

Ender replied, "True. I've seen worlds you can never imagine. Species with one heart and some with eighteen. But I have to say I agree with you. Some of the best."

Declan heard his brothers yelling again. Calling his name. He hurried closer to Ender. "You know, maybe in another plane of existence or whatever...*we* could be friends."

The drone hovered closer. "No. But you know what? For some reason, my Creator wants to be your f...f...ugh, I can't say it."

"Friend? Your Creator?"

"Yeah, weird, right? But you should read His book sometime. Talk to Him. Maybe you could find everything you want in Him."

"His book? Does it have a movie version?"

The drone scoffed. "Oh my…"

"Declan!" Quinn called. "Where are you?"

They'd be coming around the corner any second, so Declan tried to think of what to say, but…

"Bye, Declan." The drone dropped to the ground.

Declan gasped and knelt at it. "Ender! Ender!" He knocked on it, looking into its sensors. Nothing but cold steel and dark plastic.

And Quinn ran up, huffing. "You okay? Did it malfunction?"

Declan sighed and stood up, eyes wide and sad. He thought about what Ender had said. He had so many more questions. Had he been serious about texting? He hoped so, but somehow he knew it wasn't true. Ender had served his purpose and moved on to the next. He was gone. If he never texted, though, Declan would at least try to track down that book he was talking about. "Nah. I just dropped it. Sorry."

Quinn gave an annoyed look but shrugged it off. "You got it? Or should I fly it home?"

"I got it." He lugged it up and followed Quinn back to Trevor. He smiled at the goofy kid, remembering his brick throwing skills. He had to give him credit for that. Then he saw the caged squirrel.

"What are we doing with this squirrel?"

Declan's brothers looked at him, obviously surprised at his use of the word 'we.'

After the surprise wore off, Trevor pointed his hook at the squirrel. "We're going to tag it with a GPS and then track it to all ith hiding spoth. Then we're going to thteal all ith nuth."

Declan arched his brow. "Couldn't we just go to the Food O'Rama and get our own bag of…never mind. You know what? That sounds like fun. I'm in."

Made in the USA
Monee, IL
02 June 2020